SPECIAL MESSAGE TO READERS

This book is published under the auspices of

THE ULVERSCROFT FOUNDATION

(registered charity No. 264873 UK)

Established in 1972 to provide funds for research, diagnosis and treatment of eye diseases. Examples of contributions made are: —

A Children's Assessment Unit at Moorfield's Hospital, London.

•

Twin operating theatres at the Western Ophthalmic Hospital, London.

•

A Chair of Ophthalmology at the Royal Australian College of Ophthalmologists.

•

The Ulverscroft Children's Eye Unit at the Great Ormond Street Hospital For Sick Children, London.

You can help further the work of the Foundation by making a donation or leaving a legacy. Every contribution, no matter how small, is received with gratitude. Please write for details to:

THE ULVERSCROFT FOUNDATION,
The Green, Bradgate Road, Anstey,
Leicester LE7 7FU, England.
Telephone: (0116) 236 4325

In Australia write to:

THE ULVERSCROFT FOUNDATION,
c/o The Royal Australian College of Ophthalmologists,
27, Commonwealth Street, Sydney,
N.S.W. 2010.

BROKEN MELODY

When Rachel is employed as secretary to famous pianist Rick Corelli, she arrives at his beautiful home in Cornwall. But life at Gull Cliff is not so idyllic. There is the musician's unfriendly manager; the intimidating grandmother ruling the household; the enmity between Rick and his brother; and dark whispers about Rick's dead wife, mother of his two difficult children. Above all, can Rachel help falling in love with this gifted, troubled, fascinating man?

Books by Mavis Thomas
in the Linford Romance Library:

HOME IS WHERE THE HEART IS
THE SUNSHINE DAYS

MAVIS THOMAS

BROKEN MELODY

Complete and Unabridged

LINFORD
Leicester

First Linford Edition
published 2000

British Library CIP Data

Thomas, Mavis
Broken melody.—Large print ed.—
Linford romance library
1. Love stories
2. Large type books
I. Title
823.9′14 [F]

ISBN 0–7089–5705–6

Published by
F. A. Thorpe (Publishing)
Anstey, Leicestershire

Set by Words & Graphics Ltd.
Anstey, Leicestershire
Printed and bound in Great Britain by
T. J. International Ltd., Padstow, Cornwall

This book is printed on acid-free paper

1

'Good afternoon! I've an appointment to see Mrs. Nicholson, about the secretarial job. Er — three o'clock?'

The young lady at Reception in the Talbot Hotel vestibule returned my smile pleasantly as she referred to a dismayingly long list of names. 'Miss Thornton, yes? You're rather early.'

'I know! *And* I've been walking up and down outside,' I confessed.

Her smile this time was quite sympathetic. Indeed, I had dallied and dawdled from the bus stop, and still spent the last twenty minutes examining the dusty London trees around Talbot Square, resplendent in their fresh leaves. This late-Spring day had turned itself into sudden midsummer, so I was much too warm in my formal dark suit — and the shoes that went with it were torturing my toes.

'Well, I think you're in luck,' the friendly receptionist said. 'It looks as though the previous applicant is leaving already, so Mrs. Nicholson is just free. So go straight through, Miss Thornton! — that table in the corner.'

I passed by the 'previous applicant' on my way across the carpet between the groups of seats and tubs of plants. We eyed each other defensively.

'Good afternoon,' I started again. 'I've an appointment for three o'clock — '

'Ah yes! Hallo there!' The occupant of the corner seat rose at once to extend a cordial hand. 'You must be Rachel Thornton? — you're early, but never mind. Much better to be early than late. Now sit down, can I order you some tea? . . . it's so *warm* today, isn't it? . . . '

Whatever I had expected, somehow I found reality surprising. Despite that informal greeting, the piercing blue of her eyes behind designer-framed glasses was examining me with shrewd intensity, from my breeze-tossed hair and warm freckled forehead to the shine on those excruciating shoes. She was tall, straight-backed, dressed in stylish black relieved by a rope of antique amber. Once upon a time her face must have been quite beautiful — and in advanced age it was still handsome. Her upswept hair was snow-white: if it came to guessing *how* far her age might be advanced, I was utterly baffled.

'Well now,' she was commencing briskly, 'one question first, to save wasting time for both of us! If I chose you for this position, you're quite sure you could move to Cornwall for several weeks?'

I had said so already in my letter of application. Now I said again, I was ready, willing and able. She nodded, still intently appraising me.

'Good. St. Denna is a pretty place, but we're secluded. No bright lights and big shops. You wouldn't mind that?'

'I really wouldn't,' I insisted, and she

nodded again, seeming to believe me. It was the prelude to a long session of questions and answers — which centred far more on my personal history than on business qualifications.

In fact, it was quite a sad family saga I had to relate: my mother died while I was a child, my father suffered a severe stroke when barely middle-aged — and so I had been for some while both mother and father to my much younger sister Samantha. Long ago my studies at the South London Music Academy were exchanged for mundane but steady office jobs, for visits to Pa at the Nursing Home where he was resident, for all the pressing home responsibilities.

Today, I was twenty-six and Sam just twelve. It worried me that the sister so dear to me — always a painfully timid 'ugly duckling' with her strong-lensed glasses and over-large front teeth — made no friends at school, missed out on her classmates' swimming parties or birthday jaunts, and seemed to delight solely in her weekly piano lessons with Miss Crocker.

'Real talent, lots of promise . . . but *no* confidence,' the earnest little music-teacher had told me several times. It seemed to sum up Sam's small sad life in a nutshell.

So it was greatly for my sister's sake that I had seized on an advertisement found for me by my long-standing friend Dawn Walker, who most conveniently worked in an Employment Bureau. There weren't, she assured me, many openings akin to this! —

> '*Competent secretary required for the summer, knowledge of classical music helpful. Also assist with two young children. Coastal location in Cornwall, own child age seven upwards welcome. Accommodation plus generous salary. Interviewing in London — Mrs. Iris Nicholson.*'

It was this same Mrs. Nichsolson who was putting me through something like a third degree in the hotel coffee-lounge. Dawn was maybe right in advising, 'The job sounds perfect for you, just *sell* yourself!' . . . but selling anything at all to Iris Nicholson was another matter.

'There's no problem about leaving London,' I was explaining further, 'because I've an Aunt coming from Canada in a few days, she'd be delighted to take over the house! I think — I'm sure — it would do my sister good to have a complete change. She's very shy. No trouble at all, but people often don't understand her — '

'She's just twelve, you said? Do you have a photograph?'

I passed over one of the snapshots Dawn took on Sam's recent birthday: there she was, gawkily tall, beanpole thin, her sandy hair severely braided, leaning on our well-worn piano among a scattering of sheet music. Beside her, drawn up to my full five-feet-two. I was beaming broadly as though for both of us.

Mrs. Nicholson commented, 'She plays the piano too? — well, that's very nice,' and moved straight on to references.

'They're here. I've been at the Insurance Office a year, but they cut down staff and I was one of the cuts. I'm pretty useless with computers!' I admitted. 'I can do audio dictation — if you don't dictate too fast — '

'You wouldn't be working for *me*. Dear me, no!' she dismissed that idea. 'It's Mr. Corelli who'll need the secretary. He's working on a book related to classical music, and most of all he'll need *intelligence* and *accuracy*. He should be doing these interviews himself to explain properly, but at present he's staying in Italy with his relatives . . . '

Disturbed by the name and location, I admitted again, 'Sorry, I'm not good at languages either!'

'But you're refreshingly honest.' She smiled at me quite encouragingly. 'Don't worry about languages. He's my grandson Rick — my daughter's boy.' She prompted. 'Riccardo Corelli?'

The name was familiar to me. And so it should be, as an erstwhile music student, a collector of top-class recordings. Occurring here and now, it was unexpected enough to set me babbling foolishly.

'Oh, you don't mean — not THE Riccardo Corelli? — oh, I've collected all his piano recordings! I tried to take Sam to hear him once in London but we couldn't get seats! — '

'That's the one!' She seemed pleased by my reaction to the name. 'Rick is writing about his career — his various tours, you'd find it interesting. And they're *his* little girls who'll need supervising. Lively young monkeys, I warn you! . . . '

It was hard now to take in any more details beyond the identity of the man she called so composedly 'Rick'. Bemused, I sat there while she followed up a couple of my references immediately by phone. After that she handed me a photograph of the Corelli home at St. Denna: the big house, called romantically 'Gull Cliff', was perched high above an unspoiled rocky shore. It looked more like an expensive hotel, a spread of grey and white walls and blue shutters.

At last she began pushing my papers back into a businesslike folder, and thanked me for coming.

'This all seems very satisfactory, Miss — it's Rachel, isn't it? I'll let you know. And I can tell you, you're certainly on my short list!'

Somehow I was back in the street. Busy traffic was still passing. Sunshine still glorified the London trees.

I rushed for a local commuter train, packed and stuffy. All those homebound hordes looked a dejected lot! — from banks, maybe, or stock-brokers. Of course, not everyone could aspire to live in a fabulous clifftop house and work on the memoirs of a famous musician.

Warm and breathless, I reached home

just as my sister was opening the gate, clutching her school bag and music-case. On Fridays she went straight from school to Miss Crocker.

'Sammy, sorry I'm so late, that interview just went on and on! — '

'It's all right. I've just got here. I was doing the new piece, Miss Crocker let me stay on ten minutes — I'm on page 4 now, the *molto crescendo* with all the big chords . . . '

As we went inside, she was obviously far more interested in Chopin than in a possible removal to Cornwall.

Here in Bannister Close, London S.W., hard by the eternally congested traffic along the High Road, we were a fairly quiet backwater of terraced houses, elderly and solid with neat squares of garden. It was pleasant and unremarkable. For as long as I could remember it had been home.

Thankfully dumping my 'interview gear' in exchange for jeans and a baggy top, I started making Sam's tea in the small familiar kitchen. I enquired, 'Much homework for the weekend, Sammy?'

'Um. Horrible science stuff.' She pulled a face.

'Well, try to do some of it before you start on the piano!'

She didn't ask about the interview, except for 'What was she like?' and 'Were there lots of others there?' I knew she hoped I *wouldn't* get the job . . . and for that reason, on the spur of the moment, I saved up the magical Corelli name as a possible 'carrot' for future use if needed. *If* ever it was needed.

There were two more things to do urgently. The first was in the sitting-room, where from the shelves housing my collection I chose a couple of CDs.

'*Corelli Plays Chopin*' the first was called. '*The Living Piano of Riccardo Corelli*', another announced grandly. I knew each note of the music, but today I was more interested in the photographs of a very dark, very serious face that gazed broodingly back at me. Those intense black eyes especially, the sensitive mouth and high artistic brow, made a striking portrait. It was a hauntingly good-looking face in its darkly Mediterranean way . . .

The second thing to do was phone Dawn — but she forestalled me, arriving on the doorstep bright and bubbly as always.

'Hi, Sam, how are you? . . . Hi, Rachel! HOW did it go? . . . '

She was on her way home from work to the nearby flat that was hers and Robbie's, her husband of less than a year. We went back a long way, Dawn and I. We had shared many highs and lows. Always, through my times of family trauma, she had given me her warmest support.

I said guardedly, 'It went all right. I think! I'm on her short list — only how long *is* a short list?'

'Who knows? Sounds good to me!' She flashed me her bright smile. 'What was Mrs. Thingy like? She sounded a bit bossy on the phone!'

'She's much *older* than I expected. I quite liked her. But anyway, I wouldn't work for her personally. Dawn, you won't believe this . . . ' I marched her through to that same corner of the other room, to display the photograph. 'He's her grandson, she calls him Rick. He's writing a book, so — he needs a typist . . . '

Her reactions somewhat resembled mine in the Talbot Hotel. She said feebly, 'Him? You'd be working for *him*?'

Side by side we gazed at that striking portrait. It was Dawn who managed to put the situation into words.

'Well. All I can say is — *wow*!'

I felt that *wow* summed up everything rather well.

* * *

On the Sunday after the interview, my Aunt and Uncle flew in from Canada. Sam and I collected them from the evening melee of the airport. Somehow all of us and all their luggage was squeezed into my car for the journey home, nearly bursting its seams or its gaskets.

It was a good many years since I last met up with my mother's older sister Doreen: after losing her first husband she had later married a widower, Greg Marshall, with a teenage family in Toronto. My brisk and businesslike Aunt took her stepmother commitments very seriously, and took firm charge of his distant household.

This summer, Doreen and Greg were seizing the chance of a prolonged trip to England — partly holiday, partly connected with Greg's business interests.

'It's so lovely to see you,' I told Doreen yet again as we lingered before bed over a sandwich supper. 'And you look *just* the same!'

People used to say I strongly resembled her, and maybe it was true. She really did look exactly as I remembered her, short and square and determined, her hair still chestnut, her hazel-brown eyes as sharp as when, in years past, Sister Doreen Clarke was a force to beware in various hospital wards.

Now, Mrs. Doreen Marshall smiled across at me as she gave a sharp nudge to Greg, sprawling his six-feet-plus sleepily on the sofa.

'You look the same too, Rachel. Despite all the problems you've had with your poor father. I just wish your Mum could see how you've kept this house so nicely — and the way you're bringing up Sammy.'

My throat ached momentarily, because across all the years my mother's loss still was pain unhealed.

'I'm doing my best for Sam. But I'm really worried about her. She's so quiet, people think she's sulky or rude — you could see, she didn't say two words to you! — '

'Oh.' Doreen dismissed this as a minor problem. 'Most kids get moody.

It'll be just a phase, she'll outgrow it.'

I wasn't at all sure of that. I tried to explain. 'She's so thin and peaky too — she isn't happy at school, she'd rather practise her piano exercises than make friends or go out. Well, that's partly why I've just applied for this *amazing* job! . . . '

I had been waiting for a chance to discuss that. Understandably the Marshalls were surprised — and also impressed. Greg said he didn't know about music or musicians, but a good job was worth grabbing: Doreen agreed with me that a spell by a grey and gold and sapphire Cornish shore, the stimulation of new surroundings and new faces, might work wonders for Sam. And as for 'house-sitting', it would suit my relatives ideally to use Bannister Close as a base during their stay.

After that, we went to our beds. Expecting scarcely to doze, I slept like a log. In the morning it was a mad rush to see Sam off on her reluctant way to school.

My plan was to take Aunt Doreen to The Willows Nursing Home today, to see if Pa recognised her. But while the visitors were having a very belated breakfast, the phone rang. A voice instantly familiar came to me like a bolt from the blue.

'Miss Thornton? — Mrs. Nicholson! . . . I'm back at St. Denna, such a relief to get away from London . . . ' She wasted no more time on pleasantries. 'Well now, you've had time to think about the job, and so have I. My short list is reduced to two names. And I'd prefer you to the other young lady. She doesn't have your child-care experience.'

There was a moment of complete silence before I asked in disbelief. 'You've chosen *me*, from all the others? I did tell you I'm not really a top-class secretary! — '

'Rachel, *do* you want this job?'

'Yes! Yes please!'

'I'm glad to hear it. As for qualifications, there's much more to life than a frantic typing speed. So when could you start? — would next week be too soon for you?'

'Next *week*? . . . I could probably manage — I could try! — '

'Excellent! I'll post confirmation off today. I want you nicely settled in before my grandson gets here — Rick is due back from Italy any time, and he'll want to start work on the book right away. Now, my dear, any problems at all, just phone me! I'm looking forward to you and your sister joining us, Rachel.'

Having said her piece, she wasted neither time nor money hanging on the phone line. These last moments seemed like a dream — but it *was* no dream! Had I not just answered that most businesslike question, 'When could you start? . . . '

I rushed to broadcast the news to Doreen and Greg, almost choking them at their belated breakfast table.

Then I rang Dawn — who triumphed justifiably, 'Yippee! — but didn't I *say* it was in the bag?'

Lingering disbelief, huge excitement, must soon give way to down-to-earth preparations, because moving to Cornwall in these few days would be the maddest of rushes. But first came today's visit to Pa: it was very important, now, that he should recognise Doreen — and I was delighted that remembrance did filter through. It mattered very much that he had 'family' close by. She was soon chatting to him in her direct fashion, even buttonholing a nurse to offer opinions on his diet and medication.

I did try to tell him Sam and I would be staying a while by the sea. If he got the impression it was a holiday, that was no problem. I was just deeply relieved to be leaving him in such good hands.

From then onwards came that whirl of preparations. There was Sam's school, the not very easy task of explaining her future absence: there was Miss Crocker, who murmured in awe about superb Corelli performances — 'unsurpassed, unsurpassable!' There were three shopping sessions for clothes that wouldn't disgrace me at Gull Cliff: modelling to an amused Dawn and Aunt Doreen, I pointed out, 'You can't expect *the* Mr. Corelli to dictate his epic to a frump!'

Doreen hoped the man would emerge from his music long enough to pay my salary on time, as I was pre-spending it. Dawn said, 'Rachel, from the looks of *the* Mr. Corelli, he won't care if you wear a black plastic sack so long as you can spell Rachmaninov.' Which could be near the truth.

A couple of times I spoke to Mrs. Nicholson, and she was brisk and helpful. It was on the eve of departure, after a 'send-off' meal kindly hosted by Dawn and Robbie, that Sam asked me plaintively, 'Can we take the piano with us?'

'Take the — ? Sammy, talk sense!'

'Well, we could have it sent. In a van. Why can't we?'

'I don't think so. Anyway, there'll be pianos there, for sure!'

'But he won't let me near his ones, will he?' she challenged. The 'carrot' of my new employer's identity so far had been a dismal failure. Perhaps she couldn't fully believe it — any more than I could.

I agreed, 'Maybe not. But there'll be the children for company — and when you do go back to Miss Crocker you'll have so much to tell her! — '

There I stopped. Her eyes behind their glasses were brimming over.

Dawn had lingered to say goodbye. When she handed Sam a little teddy-bear wearing a teeshirt emblazoned *GOOD LUCK* my sister bore it off upstairs fairly in a flood of tears.

In the porch I frowned at the sunset behind familiar slate roofs.

'Dawn — do you think I'm doing the right thing?'

'Of course you are.' For a moment

my friend held me, her cheek against mine. 'Tomorrow's waiting for you — and for Sam. It's going to be wonderful!'

I gave her a grateful squeeze. I agreed, 'I think so too! I'll write to you, I promise. I'll ring you.'

* * *

That night certainly I didn't sleep like a log. Very early I was astir, loading up the car with what seemed like our entire worldly possessions. Aunt Doreen, already completely at home in my kitchen, insisted on serving up a cooked breakfast: 'Rushing away on an empty stomach is no good to anyone!' was her maxim.

Sam ate next to nothing and said next to nothing. In the end, I hurried over the moment of leaving to avoid upsetting her still more.

After that, there was just the car becoming more and more hot and cramped under a clear sky blazing with sunshine more akin to mid-July than late May. There were the roads of Southern England stretching on dustily ahead for ever. Worst of all, there was Sam's propensity for car-sickness on long journeys. I had hoped it was outgrown. It wasn't outgrown.

We made a number of emergency stops, dallying at service stations for drinks of water and rest periods: they slowed our progress greatly but didn't much help the sufferer. It was quite late in the afternoon when she finally fell asleep, curled on the back seat, her head pillowed on a bumpy holdall. I put my foot down then, more concerned about teetering luggage and making up lost time than the beautiful verdant country of Devonshire spread around us.

Still we were running very late when the Cornish border was crossed. The final exhausting miles at last brought the signpost I had been seeking. An almost unreal sunset, deepest pink shaded to gold, was just fading into twilight when a winding branch-road announced *WELCOME TO ST. DENNA.* Ahead of us was a steep descent to an unexpected valley between the towering ramparts of cliffs: clusters of lighted houses, a few small shops, a glimpse of mysteriously shadowed ocean.

'Sammy,' I called softly. 'Sam, wake up! — Just *look* at this place!'

Mrs. Nicholson's restrained photograph had given no real idea of all this dramatic grandeur. As we turned on to an unmade track labelled 'Gull Cliff', struggling and bumping up still higher, I saw at the summit was the spreading bulk of a big house. Its lights revealed a a glimpse of terraced gardens in the dusk.

An ornate scrollwork gateway gave us entrance to a paved courtyard, centred by a circular lily-pool. Stone urns spilled cascades of flowers. The air was cool and clean. From somewhere far below I could hear the wash and hiss of an unsleeping tide.

For a moment I just sat there. I was

conscious only of sheer awe.

'Rachel, is that you? . . . We were getting really worried about you! . . . '

Mrs. Nicholson's snow-white hair showed up in the gloom, her tall spare figure, a welcoming smile tempered by my gross disregard of punctuality. I apologised. 'I'm sorry we're so late. Sammy wasn't well, she just *isn't* a good traveller!'

She peered in at my sister, who was blearily clawing hair from her face.

'Dear me! Yes, I see what you mean. Never mind, Samantha, we'll soon have you feeling better! . . . Liz, come along, don't dawdle when there's work to do! . . . '

She looked round sharply at the girl who had followed her from the house: maybe eighteen or nineteen, with a mass of spiral-permed hair and a pretty, sulky face. Liz Banner, she explained, was the daughter of a friend of a friend — 'I've commandeered her for the summer to help out, I'm not so young as I was — and we'll all have our hands plenty full when Rick arrives! . . . Liz, see which of these things Miss Thornton needs tonight, then she can garage her car and fetch the rest in tomorrow. Hurry up, we don't want to stand here all night!'

With Iris Nicholson in charge, one didn't dilly-dally. I backed the car under cover, while Liz trundled away the big wheeled suitcase. I put a reassuring arm around Sam, silent and shivering, to help her inside.

'That's right. Come along, Samantha, no-one's going to eat you.' Mrs. Nicholson was giving her that head-to-toe scrutiny I well remembered, but she patted her shoulder in kindly fashion. 'Rinse your face in cold water, then get straight to bed. You'll be fighting fit tomorrow!'

Busy with Sam, my first impressions of the house were blurred. A wide hall, floored with black and white mosaic tiles, was furnished austerely with antique sit-up-and-beg upholstered chairs — and a fascinating array of framed concert programmes along one wall. A curve of staircase led to a gallery-landing with several stained-wood doors. The bathroom we were shown, all pale buff and pastel turquoise, looked too beautiful to be contaminated by travel-worn intruders. Finally, there was a spacious bedroom which we were evidently to share: marigold curtains and duvets, a window looking out on darkness which I realised with a thrill was actually the sea. A distant buoy or two winked warning lights to mark what must be concealed rocks or promontories.

'Sammy, isn't this all like fairyland? Won't Dawn and Aunt Doreen be green with envy when we tell them?— '

It was unwise of me to remind her of home. I left her snuggled down, almost eclipsed by her marigold covers. She was still clinging to Dawn's teddy as though it was a last link with her own world.

Washed, combed, hopefully made presentable, I found Mrs. Nicholson below waiting for me. She swept me through to a pleasant sitting-room where a low table was spread with sandwiches, a bowl of cling peaches, a jug of cream. Liz, more sulky-faced than ever in the lighted room, came in to dump down a pot of tea.

'Earl Grey. I hope that will suit you?' my hostess asked. 'I never drink anything else. Rick has coffee morning noon and night — bad for his nerves, I always tell him, but of course he pays no attention . . . '

I hastened to accept the Earl Grey. Mrs. Nicholson frowned at Liz's retreating back.

'Young people nowadays think the world owes them a living. — Well, it's nice to have you here, Rachel!' She smiled at me quite benignly. 'I hope you'll soon settle down with us. It may seem quiet now, but we're a busy household. Rick's two kiddies see to that when they're here! They're away for a few days — I sent them off on one of these 'activity' holidays, they do like activity. They're not *wild*, you understand, just high-spirited. Quite demanding.'

I muttered a diplomatic 'Ah.'

'They've had an unsettled life. Travelling around with their father . . . losing their mother a couple of years ago, poor Tina died in a very tragic accident . . . '

She talked on a while longer about the twin girls, Jade and Jenna, aged eight and a half. It did strike me she was making rather a lot of excuses for them.

'Another cup?' she offered. 'No? . . . well, perhaps you'd like to look round some of the house, then you'll be ready for bed. You must be weary.'

Weary I was, but wide awake now to the newness and strangeness all around. She showed me an impressive dining-room, with sea-blue velvet curtains, silver candle-holders, an old marble fireplace: the small 'study' where I would be working, more or less filled with bookshelves and a massive old desk: the well-equipped kitchen area where Liz was clearing up the supper things, adjoining what was called 'the morning-room', olde-worlde chintz and a family meal-table.

Nothing, nothing at all, impressed me as much as one brief glimpse of the music-room, quite sparsely furnished, utterly dominated by the gleaming bulk of Riccardo Corelli's grand piano. In the doorway I stood just gazing. Arched windows, more soft blue curtaining, bow-fronted cabinets filled with bound volumes and loose piles of sheet music — a huge old jug of flowers in the fireplace: and on the mantelpiece a silver-framed photograph of the pianist at work in this very room, a monochrome study seeming to emphasise that striking, sombre face. The dark eyes seemed directed straight across at me to ask, '*And who might you be*?'

'Mrs. Nicholson, I hope — I do hope he's not too hard to please!'

'Oh.' She patted my arm. 'Just stand up to him and you'll be all right. Just don't let him boss you around!'

Coming from her, it was amusing advice.

Over by the piano she was removing some real or imagined speck of dust. The way she touched the instrument was like a caress, as though she were reaching out to the gifted hands that could give it splendid life.

'Rick has been — quite unwell, since poor Tina died. He took the bereavement badly.' Her voice was abrupt, crushing down any excess of emotion. 'It's caused a break in his career. He turned down quite a number of concert dates.'

'Yes, I haven't heard of him lately. Just a few re-issues of recordings.'

'That's right. He spent a while in Switzerland, a long time in Italy . . . he hasn't lived here much. I suppose there are too many memories. Some years ago he was in this area with Tina and they saw this house advertised for sale. Tina fell in love with it though it was very run down. Rick bought it for her. She renamed it — previously it was called something quite ordinary . . . and she planned all the modernisations. She had good taste.'

I said softly again, 'Yes. How sad she couldn't enjoy living here.'

'She didn't even see the place completed. After she died, Rick couldn't bear to sell Gull Cliff — he asked me to move in and have all her alterations finished . . . so I gave up my own house in Surrey, it was the least I could do after all the grief and horror and misery he went through . . . '

There she pulled up short, perhaps remembering I was a stranger. She cleared her throat harshly. 'Well, while he isn't performing it's a good time to work on his book! It'll do him good to tackle a job of work. I want you to be as helpful and patient as you can, Rachel.'

'Of course. Of course I will.'

'You may not find him — easy to work with. Just do your best. His doctor said he needed 'rest and freedom from stress' — it's mainly a matter of time. We hope by the end of the summer he'll be back in full production. A few concert dates in the autumn would be nice.'

'I hope so. I really do.' I agreed warmly.

'Good. I'm glad I've made it all clear. You're a very caring young lady, Rachel — which is why I chose you to come here ahead of other people with bundles of certificates to show me! And now that's quite enough Corelli family gossip for tonight. Go and get a good night's sleep. Have you everything you need upstairs?'

I assured her I had. We exchanged pleasant good-nights. As I turned away, she added one more thing: 'Oh yes — we might soon see something of Rick's brother. But we'll cross that bridge if we come to it!'

It was my first intimation that such a person existed. Her way of phrasing the information did seem odd. I asked,

'Shall I be working for him too? Is he a musician as well?'

She answered sharply, sternly, on both counts. 'No, you won't! — and he's no musician in any serious sense. Alex is a qualified accountant. He lives in London now. He used to be Rick's manager.'

'Then — he isn't any more? I suppose there's been no 'managing' to do? — '

'Rick was obliged to dispense with his services.'

The curt answer more or less warned me to curb my curiosity. I did just that, wishing her a second 'Good night.'

By now I was exhausted enough simply to fall into my comfortable bed. At least Sam was slumbering peacefully, forgetful of all her woes.

I drifted to sleep with one last lingering thought. Haunted by the troubles and enigmas of the Corelli family, was Gull Cliff going to prove quite the paradise it seemed?

* * *

In the morning there were unfamiliar sounds abroad. The house lived up to its name, as persistent eerie sea-bird cries, mournful and strange, seemed to rise to a wild crescendo right at my bedside. I padded across to the window — and was startled by the wide and glorious vista spread below, pearly early-morning light on a wide sea, grey parapets of rock, white foam around stranded islets and pinnacles.

Sam was still sleeping, but downstairs I found the kitchen full of activity. Inevitably, Liz was being held to account for something by Mrs. Nicholson, busy and energetic as ever at barely seven a.m.

She greeted me pleasantly, 'Good morning, Rachel! Did you sleep well?'

'Like a top, thank you. And Samantha too.'

'Good,' she approved. I sensed that any other answer would receive short shrift. She suffered neither weaklings nor incompetents gladly.

Afraid of appearing idle, I went out

to the garage to retrieve some items of luggage, and surveyed the gardens barely glimpsed last night. Awkward slopes and shapes had been skilfully landscaped with rockeries and terraces of velvet-green lawn. As well, a flight of rough steps spiralled invitingly down, no doubt a private path to the shore.

Back inside, I found the hall telephone ringing persistently. As my first duty here, I picked it up.

An irate voice announced, 'Roger Ferris here. Jack and Jill activity Holidays. I'm sorry to say Jade and Jenna Corelli are causing so much trouble here that we're *not* prepared to keep them any longer! So I'm ringing to ask,' the angry Mr. Ferris swept on, 'if you'll kindly collect them. *Today*, please, before they disrupt our entire programme!'

Aware of Mrs. Nicholson coming up at a rush. I hissed at her the gist of the man's grievance. Her brow grim, she took over.

'Good morning, Mr. Ferris! This is

Jade and Jenna's Great-Grandmother. Certainly they're high spirited girls, surely you can cope with that? . . . No, I'm not interested in a refund. I'd just like the service I've paid for!' She ended curtly, 'It's NOT convenient to collect them, if you want them sent home you can deliver them yourself!'

The receiver back in place, she turned to me with a dismissive smile.

'Quite absurd. A storm in a teacup! I shall write to the Head Man and complain *very* strongly! . . . Rachel, will you come and have some breakfast? — though how Liz manages to scorch every piece of toast I'll never know . . . '

First, I flew upstairs to haul my bleary-eyed sister out of bed. It wouldn't do to be late at table and cause any more storms in teacups.

Sam ate scarcely a crumb, subdued and uneasy under Mrs. Nicholson's eye. But she did look far more presentable this morning. She answered politely that her room was 'very nice'. Not too imaginative, but it was a start.

'Well!' Mrs. Nicholson said briskly. 'You can show Samantha around, Rachel. The sooner you both get to feel at home here, the better.'

Obedient to orders, I started Sam on the 'grand tour'. The various rooms, and a pleasant conservatory with potted plants and wicker furnishings — I missed that last night — rounded her eyes in wonder but evoked little comment. In the 'study', I lingered to try out the electronic typewriter, which seemed to possess a baleful will of its own. Beside it were two audio tapes that had been removed from a package with an Italian stamp, labelled '*Chapt.1*' and '*Chapt.1 Amendments*'.

'Are you going to do them now?' Sam asked without much interest.

'I'm not sure. I don't know how he'll want them done — so perhaps I'll wait till he comes. Let's look round some more!'

I couldn't avoid letting her glimpse the music-room, where she froze into utter reverence. She breathed 'That photo — it's the *same* as . . . well, nearly the same . . . '

'Of course. It's the same man, Sammy. I told you.'

'Oh!' she whispered. It seemed this was the first time understanding really dawned.

I hastened to add, 'But I'm sure we mustn't touch anything in here — which means no, you can't try out the piano! Come on, let's look round the garden.'

She followed me reluctantly into the fresh air. As we explored, there was evident some errant grass and weeds here and there: I wondered, was it part of Liz's job or mine to look after garden maintenance? . . .

'A bus,' Sam said casually. 'Coming up the hill.'

'A *bus*? — oh no, a mini-bus labelled 'Jack and Jill'! Sam, this means trouble! Will you run in and find Mrs. Nicholson?'

The vehicle pulled up smartly on the driveway and its driver began banging doors and unloading luggage with much unnecessary noise. I called to him brightly, 'Hallo! — I see you've brought the children back. Mrs. Nicholson won't be very pleased!'

With deep interest I watched Rick Corelli's daughters clamber from the vehicle. Of course, I had known they were twins — but it was startling to find them so completely alike. Peas in a pod, flowerpots on a shelf, pins in a packet, were phrases that sprang to mind. Small and slight for their age, sloe-eyed, certainly very attractive in a gipsy-like way, it didn't help that they wore identical sweaters and pink jeans, that both had bouncing tails of dark hair fastened with the same pink scrunchies. Both wore small diamonds in their ears. Both also sported glaring magenta nail varnish — no doubt applied while safely apart from their Great-Grandmother.

Until now I had been imagining almost some sort of juvenile monsters. But my first favourable impression wavered when I noticed two rudely extended lengths of tongue behind the driver's back.

Mrs. Nicholson was approaching now at a trot, so the luckless man from Jack and Jill's was likely to get more than he had bargained for. Starting to shepherd Sam back to the house, I whispered to her, 'What do you think of them?' She stuck out her lower lip expressively.

Back indoors, having dealt with Mr. Ferris, Mrs. Nicholson performed brisk introductions: 'Jade — Jenna — this is Miss Thornton. She'll be working for your Daddy and helping out here. What do you say, girls?' she prompted.

One of them dropped me an insolent curtsey. The other answered with a flood of words from which I could distinguish only 'Bon giorno!'

'*English*, if you don't mind! (Pretty well bi-lingual,' she explained to me aside, 'they use it to their advantage whenever they can — little monkeys!) . . . Girls, listen to me! — you're to do exactly what Miss Thornton says, no nonsense! And this is her sister

Samantha. Say 'hallo' nicely. I want you to be good friends.'

They chorused sweetly, 'Hallo, Samantha. Nice to meet you, Samantha. Hope you're having a good time here, Samantha.'

It dissolved into whispers and giggles, before they rioted away upstairs.

'Just high spirits,' Mrs. Nicholson said. 'Now, Rachel my dear, when Rick arrives you'll be kept busy so enjoy life while you can! Take your sister to the shops, buy the child something nice — I can't be doing with long faces around. And take the twins too, get to know them.'

Though delivered in such friendly fashion, clearly these were my orders for the day.

Sam was holed up in our room and needed coaxing to leave it, and the twins demanded a second breakfast ('Masses of toast and jam! — that holiday place food was *disgusting*,' they declared, sending a simmering Liz back to the kitchen): so it was some while later when I loaded my three passengers into the car. Jade and Jenna, whichever was which, commented that the vehicle was old, shabby, and needed a wash.

'You should see our Daddy's car. That's what you *call* a car!'

'Then when he gets here you can ride in it. Meantime, you ride in mine. In the back, please,' I instructed, 'and mind you fasten the seatbelts!'

Their Great-Grandmother nodded approval. 'Quite right, Rachel, start as you mean to go on. Goodbye, all of you, have fun! — and don't hurry back!'

Turning cautiously down the steep road towards the huddle of roots below that was St. Denna, I was aware of much wriggling, whispering and giggling on the back seat. Many of the whispers were fluent Italian, but pointedly in English were those concerning 'rabbit teeth' or 'boffin glasses'. Sitting bolt upright beside me in front, Samantha was stony-faced.

'Where do you go to school,

Samantha?' one of the girls asked sweetly.

'Near where we live. Streatham — that's sort of London.'

'We've lived in London. We didn't like it,' asserted the one with the scratch on her nose — I believed it was Jenna.

'Paris was nicer,' her sister agreed. 'Milan wasn't bad — was it, Jen?'

'New York was best. Our Daddy played in this huge theatre. They did massive ice-creams in the hotel with nuts and chocolate fudge and strawberries. I had three. I was sick four times.'

'Five,' Jade corrected. 'And Daddy called the doctor 'cos you were a funny colour. And Uncle Alex said it served you right for being greedy.'

'Trust *him*. Well, we don't have *him* around any more! . . . '

They shared an assurance far above their years. They were very bright, very intelligent. Most of all, their worldly-wise 'seen it all'/'done it all'/'been there' nonchalance was quite unnerving.

I suggested, 'You've certainly been around! — but surely nowhere is much nicer than Mrs. Nicholson's lovely house here?'

'It's not hers. It's our Daddy's. She just lives in it,' Jade corrected scathingly. 'It's *one* of his houses . . . '

I heard my sister mutter, 'Show-off!' The outing wasn't going too well.

St. Denna's narrow streets were all happily uncommercialised, with just a few 'b & b' signs, small shops with gifts and art materials, a couple of eating places. I decided, 'I need some postcards, so we'll shop first — then how about lunch?'

'That Quayside Cafe does yummy chips,' Jade conceded.

'Right! We'll have some yummy chips. I wonder if the car-park is full?'

It wasn't full. Marshalling my party off towards the shops, it struck me that the contrast couldn't have been greater: the two younger girls, so dark and lively and pretty, Sam tall and thin as a beanpole, her freckles spreading by the minute. Which reminded me, I must buy some mega-strength sun-cream for both our sakes . . .

'Look, this shop has nice cards. In here, please!' I directed.

Surrounded by a variety of pebble jewellery and shell ornaments, it took me a few minutes to pick out the nicest coloured postcards to send home. I heard the girls admiring a ship in a bottle. When I looked round again, someone was chatting to someone else at the counter, a young boy was pestering his mother for sweets — otherwise the shop was empty.

I peered behind all the display stands. The other people hadn't seen the children melt away, but melt away they had. Suddenly my heart was hammering, my hands were clammy. I started calling, 'Sammy? . . . Jade? . . . Jenna?' as panic deepened.

Outside on the sunny narrow pavement there were just a few people. Cars rounded the twists of the street in a manner potentially very dangerous.

I couldn't believe this was happening on my very first day, my very first hour in charge of the twins. Sam was usually staid and sensible — but she was in an unfamiliar place in company with two bad influences. Had anyone, in the turbulent lives of those hyper-precocious little girls, instructed them *not* to accept lifts from strangers? Would the two young madams take any notice if they had? . . .

'Excuse me! — Hallo? — ' a man's voice came to me through my nightmare haze.

He had pulled up a car just behind me, oblivious to yellow lines. He repeated, 'Excuse me!' and leant across. 'If it's the Corelli kids you're looking for — '

'Oh *yes*! Do you know them? — Have you seen them? I — I just turned my back for one moment — '

'Fatal mistake. Never turn your back on them,' he advised gravely. 'On a rattlesnake or a tiger, yes maybe! . . . Look, it's all right, no need to get upset. I just passed the twins sitting on a railing with another girl — quite safe and sound. I was stopping to sort them out, in case they'd come down here on their own.'

I was trembling now with quite overwhelming relief as I shook my head. 'They're not alone. I'm supposed to be in charge of them.'

'You are? Hard luck!' he sympathised.

As he uncoiled his considerable height from the car, suddenly I was startled by the impression of a stranger who didn't quite look like a stranger. Distinctly there was an image of the commanding portrait in the music-room at Gull Cliff — but with one major difference, because the eyes meeting mine with a gentle, kind, amused smile were an unexpected pale ice-blue. As well, at second glance his face was less striking, less vivid.

I blurted out, 'Sorry if I was staring. Just for a moment I thought you were — '

'No, I can't lay claim to that honour.' He didn't seem at all surprised or disturbed. 'Shall I show you where the kids are?'

Eagerly enough I followed on. Panic wouldn't quite disperse until the children were actually in sight.

And they were, the next moment. Jade and Jenna were perched jauntily on someone's high garden railing, taunting Sam below, 'Come on up, it's easy-peasy! — dare you! — dare you!'

Then the two voices changed their tune suddenly: 'Oh no, *not* Uncle Alex! . . . you're not supposed to be here! — we know!' they shrilled at him aggressively. 'Our Daddy said we're not to speak to you, never ever ever! — '

At a less fraught moment I would have realised before now a very obvious truth. I blurted out again, 'How silly of me — of course, you're just his brother!'

Alex Corelli agreed, still without apparent offence, 'That sums it up exactly.'

He was already hooking the twins down from their perch, no simple matter with their vigorous protests. By now, my vast relief had turned to anger, and I gave them a brief but pointed lecture — which left the bold gaze of Jade and Jenna utterly unchastened. Sam stood by, a picture of silent misery.

'As you've behaved so badly,' I finished up, 'we're going straight home!'

'That's not fair! You said we'd have lunch. Great-Gran said we could stay out for hours — '

'We will another day. When you learn how to behave yourselves!'

Their Uncle nodded approvingly. I looked up at him as we started back towards the car-park, still indescribably grateful for his rescue from a nightmare.

'I really can't thank you enough. And in case you're wondering — Mrs. Nicholson advertised for a secretary for Mr. Corelli. I'm Rachel Thornton, and I'm it! That's for Riccardo Corelli, of course — '

'Of course,' he said gravely. 'And Gran threw in 'look after two charming children' as an extra? — sounds just like her. She doesn't miss a trick. Nor do they, as you'll discover! . . . Look, I'm driving up to the house anyway, shall I nip back for my car and follow close behind you — in case they jump out along the way?'

'Well, thanks. Though I'm sure they wouldn't — '

'With the twins, never be sure.' He quoted their own phrase, 'Never ever ever!'

His smile was warm, humorous, comforting. I asked. 'Are you going to stay at Gull Cliff? Mrs. Nicholson said — '

I was within an inch of disclosing that his Grandmother called him 'a bridge to be crossed if we came to it.'

'I'll be staying there a while, yes. If they let me.'

I couldn't begin to understand that rather strange answer. I just hoped he would stay.

2

Our small motorcade mounted the steep road and the pebbly track. Inevitably Mrs. Nicholson was on hand to greet us: 'Well, you're back very early! — did you have a good time?'

'No, we didn't! — *she* wouldn't let us have lunch! — or spend our money!' the twins chorused.

But their grievances went unheeded, because she had seen now the second car pulling up behind mine. I saw her face change, to express as much dismay as her self-control ever allowed.

'Alex,' she greeted him, 'you know I'm always pleased to see you, but — you do know we're expecting Rick here any day now?'

'I know. You said in your letter. But the auditing job finished early, and Bill Parsons can't discuss a partnership till late August, so — well, I'm here!'

'I'm really *not* sure it's a good idea. You and your brother under the same roof . . . '

Much intrigued, but unwilling to intrude on these family problems, I swept the children off to the house. The twins clattered straight to the kitchen to give out orders: 'Liz, we're starving! — we want spaghetti and lots of chips! . . . and if you burn them we'll tell Great-Gran! . . . '

Sam had escaped to the haven of our bedroom. By now I was quite uneasy about the effect the Corelli girls might have on my quiet young sister. As for this morning's incident, some deep thought decided me against reporting it — because maybe I was partly to blame for taking too much for granted. In future, as Alex Corelli had warned me, I would take absolutely nothing for granted.

In the study I had another try-out with the unfamiliar typewriter, which surely had some malevolent 'bug' in its inner electronics. Eventually I hid the thing under its cover and sought the big kitchen, anxious to earn my keep somehow. Liz Banner seemed to exist in a permanent welter of sulks and backlogged chores, and on this sunny day I felt sorry for her.

'Sorry about that extra meal for the children.' I apologised. 'Do you cope with everything here all on your own?'

'There's the Bassetts, they live down in St. Denna. Usually she comes in to clean, only she's away with some sick relative. He does the garden, but he's busted his foot. So — '

'Too bad. Look, I'll do that salad. You pop outside for a breather!'

'Shall I? Do you mind? Only Mrs. N nags me rotten if — '

'I'm sure she won't mind,' I assured her.

Another case of misplaced confidence. Through the kitchen window I saw Liz settle down happily on a garden bench, rolling up her top to exhibit a bare midriff. Only moments later came Mrs. Nicholson's unmistakable tones.

'Elizabeth Banner. I don't pay you good money to loll around half naked when there's work to be done . . . '

It would take some while to get used to this household. More and more, as my first day wore on, I felt alone, puzzled, out of my depth. I looked in vain for Alex, who had been so friendly and comforting. I found only Sam, on the verge of tears.

'That bossy old woman! — I was only just looking in the music-room, just *looking* and — wondering what Miss Crocker would say — '

'Sammy. Didn't I tell you to keep well away?'

'I wasn't doing any harm,' she insisted. 'She came in and caught me. She went raving mad!'

I did my best to console her, and we stayed upstairs together to write letters home. It was only a temporary solution.

Presently came the evening meal,

long and awkward, at the formal table in the dining-room. Mrs. Nicholson presided in regal fashion at the head. The twins, two appealing innocents in lemon-yellow, smiled across at me sweetly — with still that glint of devilry in those black Southern eyes.

Jade asked primly, 'Where did you disappear to, Miss Thornton? We were hoping you'd take us to the beach. Weren't we, Jen?'

'Yes, 'cos Great-Gran says we mustn't ever go down on our own,' her sister agreed with soulful virtue.

'Tomorrow,' I promised rashly.

I caught a sideways glance from Alex that plainly said, 'You'll regret it!'

The conversation round the table wasn't too inspiring. Mrs. Nicholson found fault with most of Liz's offerings — and when we reached the butter-scotch whip stage she, of course, had to get the lumpy portion. The twins eventually began a long account of a gory local legend, '*The Lady of St. Denna*', directed especially at Sam.

The 'Lady' had been forsaken by her beloved, and soon afterwards he and his boat were torn apart by St. Denna's treacherous rocks. All one night she wandered the clifftops, her long hair streaming in the moonlight, until at dawn she flung herself down to join him in the boiling surf.

'So if you hear strange noises in the night,' Jenna warned Sam dramatically, 'don't ever look through the window. It'll be The Lady's ghost wandering and sobbing before it jumps into the sea!'

'And anyone who sees her,' Jade chimed in, 'will be horribly drownded too . . . '

It was Alex who gave a little squeeze to Sam's arm. 'Just ignore their gruesome tales, Sam! Anyway, I reckon any decent ghost could float — don't you?'

She gave him one of her shy smiles, and whispered that maybe it could.

The evening held more problems when I found I was expected to get the twins to bed. They did everything possible to try my patience, from a miniature Niagara Falls in the bathroom to trampolining contests on their beds. Afterwards, Sam was almost as hard to settle down, in her own way: she was homesick for her own bed in her own room — and her next music lesson. I could only assure her, things *must* get better.

Downstairs at last, I snapped on the study light. Outside in deepening dusk, flower-heads showed up almost luminous, there was a fragrance of newly watered leaves and drinking earth. I sat at the desk and tentatively opened a drawer: mixed with assorted stationery was an audio-tape: '*Collected Piano Classics — R. Corelli*'. From the box stared up at me again that familiar face.

There was a portable player on the desk, and dutifully I resisted the music and slotted in one of the worktapes sent by post. It was then that I heard for the first time a low voice with a distinctive foreign inflection, as arresting as the portrait. Strange, very strange, compared with the wholly homespun speech of Rick Corelli's brother? . . .

I had intended making notes, but the notebook page remained blank. Mesmerised. I sat there quiet and still, just gazing at the pictured face, just intently listening.

'Beg your pardon!' Another voice, as the door opened, hurtled me back to earth. 'I didn't know you were working.'

'I'm not really,' I said in some confusion. 'Just — listening.'

'Oh!' Alex pulled an expressively wry face, as I switched off the player almost guiltily. 'Rachel, I just wanted to say, I'm sorry about all our family undercurrents. It must be upsetting for you.'

As opposed to our formal mealtime garb, he looked now damp and dishevelled, in a washed-out teeshirt lettered incongruously KEEP SMILING. He had been hosing the flowers, he explained, in the absence of our regular gardener.

'I know, Mr. Bassett with the busted foot.' I asked abruptly, waving a hand at the tapeplayer, 'Sorry to be nosy, but — why does your brother sound like *him* and you sound like *you*?'

He smiled at the odd question. 'Puzzles you, does it? The answer is, our parents died when we were small — and the musical genius was snapped up by our Uncle Cesare Corelli to bring up with his family — which meant attending the Academia del Whatsit in Rome, winning every prize available. Whereas Gran took me in, I lived with her in Surrey and had a solid English education. I studied accounts, about as boring as you can get! . . . ' He added quietly, 'She was wonderful to me. I can't ever repay her. She's a very special person.'

'I'm sure,' I agreed. 'So you and — Riccardo . . . you were apart for years — and now you don't get on very well?'

'We were. And we don't.'

'So will you really have to leave when he gets here?'

'I asked the question a little wistfully. It received no real answer.

'Who can say? — I'm entitled to visit Gran if I choose, aren't I? . . . Oh, and one other thing.' He seemed to turn the conversation rather hastily. 'When Rick arrives, don't let him walk all over you! That's a hint from one who knows — I was his manager for quite a spell.'

'I know that. So was that when you quarrelled with him — ?' I started to ask. The look that came to his pleasant, gentle face, suddenly stern and secretive, warned me to leave that be. I amended, 'Does he have a manager now?'

'He hasn't needed anyone for a while — but he's just acquired a brand new one. I gather they've been together in Italy, and he's bringing her back here to stay. — Help, I'm dripping on Gran's carpet, she'll slay me!'

He gave me a parting smile. It was, as I had noted before, a nice smile.

Of course, it wasn't my business why this apparently easy-going man had fallen out so seriously with his famous brother. Perhaps it was that very fame at the bottom of it? Perhaps, despite his comments sounding mostly just wry and humorous, Alex really nursed a bitter jealousy? Or maybe he had simply wearied of being on the receiving end of too much artistic temperament? . . .

I switched on the tape again, to hear more of the voice that had so enthralled me. But this time it was quickly interrupted by a second recorded voice in the background — a feminine voice attractively husky: 'Ricco, sweetie, *are* we going out today or are you still doing that boring book? . . . '

There the tape cut off. After a moment it resumed, but somehow I didn't care to listen any further.

Still in my mind were Alex's words

about the new manager: 'He's bringing *her* back here with him to stay . . . '

* * *

The following morning brought me tidings of a distinctly 'good news'/'bad news' nature. The good side was that next week the twins would attend a day-and-boarding school a couple of miles distant, called The Heights. Mrs. Nicholson told me, 'Miss Jesmond — the Principal there — is a friend of mine and we have a little arrangement for when the girls stay with me.' (I felt probably Mrs. Nicholson had 'little arrangements' with more or less everyone.)

The Heights sounded like a blessed relief, but there was a reverse side. It would be my duty to take and fetch Jade and Jenna. Their Great-Grandmother added brightly, 'I'm sure Miss Jesmond would accept Samantha too, if I have a word?' She muttered in disapproval when I declined, hinting at what happened to 'idle hands'.

That same morning, slipping off with Sam quietly to St. Denna,I used up a small fortune in change ringing Aunt Doreen at home, and Dawn at work. Both eagerly digested details and gave their opinions, 'There may be snags, but *give it a chance*!'

Of course, I was prepared to do that. This difficult introductory time at Gull Cliff just had to be got through somehow.

And as the days of my first week moved on, gradually the surroundings did become more familiar, I grew more used to the important task of keeping on the right side of Mrs. Nicholson, to the atmosphere of the big beautiful house so strangely empty of human warmth. Unfortunately Sam remained still a very round peg in a very square hole: the chief new delight of the twins — besides leading me a general dance — seemed to be trying hard to get her in their Great-Grandmother's bad books. All too often, they succeeded.

Nor did it help that the weather turned dull and damp, so diversionary beach visits had to be postponed. On a couple of afternoons Alex and I took the three girls out by car, once to Penmoryn to see a Disney film. The twins called it 'dead boring'. Each time, Alex quietly offered me his company, his help, his support.

He was easy to know, easy to be with. He went his own unflappable and good-humoured way: he spent long hours working around the garden, occasionally he tuned a guitar to render cheery versions of 'The Sound of Music' or something from Jerome Kern or Gershwin — which always called for a sharp remonstrance from Mrs. Nicholson. He winked at me and murmured something about 'unforgivable sacrilege.'

Summer flooded back on Friday, warm sun and a smiling sky over the sea. That meant no more postponements of the beach trip: armed with a food basket and a bundle of towels, this time I asked Alex outright, 'Please come! — I've an awful feeling you'll be needed!'

As we descended those steep rough steps from Gull Cliff, here and there the stairway had crumbled, a length of safety rail had been added. The breeze fanned out my hair, the glint of sunlight on a sudden vastness of sea dazzled my eyes. The little hidden beach we finally reached was truly beautiful: firm sand broken up by strange-shaped boulders, deep rockpools each filled with a mini-world of life — and that restless tide, a shifting field of diamond-tipped turquoise, breaking into white spray along the line of cliffs.

We found a place to spread out the towels. Nearby, a dark opening in the cliff gave entrance to a small cave, and Jenna told Sam impressively, '*That's* where they found 'The Lady', all cold and dead and wound up in seaweed. Come on in, we'll show you!'

Sam was more or less propelled inside, and of course there drifted out muffled haunting noises, 'Whooo . . . I'm a ghooost . . . whooo . . . ' I heard Sam cry out, and called sharply, 'That's enough! — all of you out!'

The twins protested, 'It was only a joke. Sam's such a scaredy-cat!'

'I'm not,' Sam said fiercely. 'I bumped my head when you pushed me — I might've broken my glasses! — '

'All right, folks, calm down,' Alex interposed. 'Competition time! — fifty pence for the best sandcastle!'

There followed a blessed lull. In amicable partnership he and I set out the picnic, Liz's doorstep sandwiches, fruit and cake, bottles of pop.

'Heigh-ho! — we deserve something stronger than lemonade.' Alex stretched his tall figure out lazily on the sand. 'Rachel, I know exactly what you're thinking. '*The kids from Hell — and I'm stuck with them for the whole summer!*' — right?'

I agreed with feeling, 'Right! Well, something like that.'

'I know. A pair of obnoxious

brats — on their good days. They've given you a hard time this week. But you realise they're trying you out, to see what they can get away with? And — it's not really their fault,' he added surprisingly.

'Not their fault to hide Sam's schoolbooks so she can't do her revision work? — or tell Mrs. Nicholson *she* broke that Chinese vase when she was nowhere near it?'

'All right, point taken. But think about it. They've been shifted from pillar to post — this hotel to that — this nanny to that au pair — oh, I've seen it happening. This year alone, they started in Italy with Rick, then Tina's sister in Norwich, now here. Mustn't that give them a serious sense of insecurity? And — losing their mother, I know what that is when you're a kid. Plus of course, they take after their Dad! — you can't blame them for *that* . . . '

I said soberly, 'Mrs. Nicholson didn't tell me how their mother died.'

'She was drowned.'

I found myself shivering. The stark words were chilling, so soon after the twins' lurid tale. I tried to ask, 'How did she . . . ? Were the children . . . ?'

'Luckily they were in England. Rick and Tina were in Italy — partly holiday but he was giving a few recitals. They had — let's say, a stormy marriage. That day there was some sort of ding-dong battle. He wouldn't go to the Lake with her. She went alone, she — didn't come back. It was the last time she was seen alive . . .'

His voice trailed off there. I murmured, 'He must really have loved Tina very much — because he still hasn't been able to start playing again?'

'He'll be starting soon. So Gran keeps saying.'

Abruptly Alex sat up. There was deepest pain transforming his face, in the blue eyes avoiding mine. I sensed far more of this tragic story was still untold.

'Sorry,' he apologised. 'This is all very dismal! The end of a life, the end of a marriage, the end of a career. Rachel, I have to say — my brother is a brilliant musician but he's a cold, awkward, impossible human being. Let's just leave it at that.'

There was no doubting he meant every word. Again the motivation of jealousy — the root of so many family feuds — came to my mind.

By now the three sandcastles were built, and the easy answer to judging them was prizes all round. The picnic was enlivened by wandering crabs and various minor squabbles, and then we had a lively shell-collecting contest. It was quite late in the afternoon when we climbed back up the rough stairway. Sam's face had gained some healthy colour, and she was holding an especially pretty shell. The twins were still grumbling because, due to the dangerous shore, we had let them only dabble their toes in the water.

The next moment, that was forgotten. They let out an excited scream.

A car was just pulling up by the

house, a long, low, gleaming-white convertible, open now to the sky, with a careless pile of very plush luggage on the back seat. A young woman of maybe thirty sat at the wheel, slender and bronzed, her pale-blonde hair caught back from a face that would have graced any model. She was appraising Gull Cliff through a trendy line in designer sunglasses.

Alex murmured to me, 'So here's Rick's new manager in the flesh. And what flesh! . . .'

I found no voice to answer. At this moment she didn't interest me. I had eyes only for the man beside her, aware of my throat suddenly dry, my hands unsteady, my heart racing.

It was the same dark compelling face I had studied in all those portraits. The hands opening the car door had wafted me so often into a world of magic.

'Ricky darling! — you're here!' Scarcely before he was out of the car, Mrs. Nicholson was enfolding him in a warm embrace. (A welcome, I recalled, she hadn't accorded Alex a few days ago.) 'It's wonderful to have you home! And you do look much better! — but why didn't you tell me you'd be here today? — '

'Sorry about that. We've been travelling around, we weren't very sure of our timings.' Again, the same unmistakable voice I had heard on the tape. I watched as he turned to the blonde driver. 'Gran, will you say hallo to Abigail? Miss Abigail Horton. Abbey, this is my Grandmother.'

'Lovely to meet you,' the girl responded, with a brief dazzle of smile, very white teeth, very blue eyes. 'Isn't this a beautiful place here?'

Mrs. Nicholson's formal, 'How do you do, Miss Horton?' was on the crisp side. From my few days' knowledge of her, I sensed her first impressions of the newcomer were less than approving.

By now Jade and Jenna had launched themselves at their father, with an enthusiasm that literally almost bowled him over. He was certainly less tall than his brother, slighter than I had imagined. There was something about him almost frail and vulnerable.

'Steady, you girls, your Daddy's tired from travelling,' Mrs. Nicholson intervened in haste. She added, with a diplomatic clearing of her throat, 'Er — Rick, I'll tell you this right away. Alex has been here a few days. And he's been really helpful to me, so please don't get upset . . . You'll let him stay on, won't you? To please me?'

He seemed about to protest, and then shrugged his shoulders. 'To please *you*. Not to please him. Just tell him to keep out of my way.'

I saw the look almost of dark menace directed from the younger brother to the elder across the sunny courtyard, over the heads of the twins who were still bouncing like jack-in-the-boxes. From Alex, keeping very well in the background, there was returned only his pleasant gentle smile.

'Dear me, and there's another introduction to make!' Their Grandmother turned the subject hastily. 'Rick, this is the young lady I engaged to do your typing work. Rachel Thornton — and her sister Samantha, who'll be company for the twins. I know you'll find Rachel a real treasure.'

My face burning, I extended a hand. It was the first time his black eyes looked into mine. His hand against mine was brief and chilly.

He said, 'Hallo. Nice to meet you.'

For some reason, the words didn't sound convincing. But I echoed brightly, 'It's very nice to meet you too, Mr. Corelli! Sam and I are real fans, we collect all your recordings — every one! — '

It was a well-meaning approach. Clearly not the right one.

'That's nice. But you're not here to form a fan club, I believe you're here to work? . . . Did you type those tapes I sent on?'

I confessed, 'I haven't actually started

on them. There were no instructions, you see, so I thought it best to wait until — '

'I don't really see the problem. I expected they'd be ready. — Abbey, shall we go inside?'

He turned away towards the house with Miss Horton. It was the clear intention of both that someone else should deal with their luggage.

For a moment I just stood there. The sun glinted on the white car.

'Don't take it personally. That's just the Rick Corelli charm for you.' Alex's quiet voice said beside me. He bent to look full in my face, his eyes full of their clear-blue kindness. 'Take a little tip from a well-wisher. Don't let it worry you!'

Standing there feeling something akin to a pricked balloon. I smiled back at him. In this household, it was very nice to have a well-wisher.

* * *

Liz grumbled darkly in the kitchen, where on that first traumatic evening I was helping her drum up a meal for eight. 'I thought this job here would be a doddle. Right by the sea — and her as old as the hills —'

'Ssh! You'd better not let her hear you say that!' I warned.

'I'd be better off working in one of those b & b places, more free time — probably less hassle! . . . Of course, I don't go much on that classical piano stuff, give me Oasis or The Spice Girls,' she confided through a cloud of steam resembling an Icelandic geyser. 'But don't you think Rick Corelli is quite something when you see him for real? Like an Italian film-star?'

'Maybe,' I said guardedly. 'Liz, shouldn't you rescue those potatoes before they explode?'

I knew Rick had disappeared with Abigail Horton down to the beach. Keeping watch via the kitchen window, I observed their return. It didn't surprise me that Abigail's long hair was looped up in a damp tail, and she hung a black satin bikini to dry over a railing. It was a *small* black satin bikini. Hardly worth hanging at all. I felt sure Mrs. Nicholson's all-seeing eyes would have spotted it.

As for the meal itself, I sat beside a much overawed Sam, and pretended to eat, and listened. It was Miss Horton who claimed the spotlight, so for once the twins were upstaged: our Cornish sea was *chilly*, she said airily, but refreshing after the journey. She contrasted it with Continental resorts where she and Rick had 'stopped off' during their leisurely drive from his Aunt and Uncle's home — Cesare and Francesca and their assorted offspring. 'Nice people, they know how to make you really welcome . . . '

Whether or not that was an intended barb for Mrs. Nicholson's frostiness, I saw it was certainly taken as one.

I helped clear the dishes and then looked for Sammy. And looked and looked, with fast growing concern.

Finally, I was horrified to glimpse her through the half-open door of the forbidden music-room. Yet again, as though we hadn't problems enough!

About to haul her away, I stopped short. She was talking to someone, very pink of face, very nervous of voice, but animated and excited as she leafed through a pile of music on the table near the piano.

'This one!' she announced. 'It's so beautiful — but I can't ever get this bit right — and Miss Crocker says — '

'Yes, it's beautiful. Show me how it goes wrong.' In sheer disbelief. I saw Rick Corelli gesturing her towards the piano. 'Go on. It's all right. Don't be afraid of it.'

'Oh, can I really? . . . ' She perched on the stool as though it was red hot, hesitantly her fingers touched the keys. She breathed, 'Oh, this is — *super* . . . '

'Nice, isn't it?' he agreed, as though to an equal colleague. My Gran keeps it maintained, but it needs using. — No, no! C sharp there . . . '

'Sorry. I — I can't do the next bit.'

'Yes, you can! Careful, now C natural . . . *con fuoco*, let's hear the fire! . . . watch the timing . . . '

It lasted only a moment. The broken snatch of Chopin drifting into the summery dusk brought Mrs. Nicholson fairly scuttling on to the scene, brushing me from the doorway.

She exclaimed, 'Oh, Ricky . . . ' and then another deflated, 'Oh! I see.'

My sister skipped off the stool like a cat caught at a cream-jug.

'I — I thought — when I heard — ' Mrs. Nicholson was still stuttering and stammering — something unknown in my experience of her. Without understanding, I was sorry for her.

Certainly she wasn't helped by her grandson's response, 'You thought wrong. And it would be nice to have some privacy in my own house.'

It seemed to me curtness quite uncalled for. He shut down the lid of the piano. As he left the room, all three of us hastened to make room for him.

Mrs. Nicholson rounded on Sam, which was perhaps understandable: 'I thought I told you, miss! — keep out of here, don't make yourself a nuisance!'

Sam actually stood her ground to protest. 'I wasn't a nuisance, he didn't *mind*! — '

'I'm very sorry, Mrs. Nicholson.' In haste I grabbed this startling new Sam by the arm. 'It won't happen again.'

'I hope it won't,' she said tartly. 'Please make sure the twins get to their beds, Rachel. I can hear them raising Cain up there!'

I yanked Sam upstairs, hissing at her that this wasn't our house, we had to obey the rules, we had to keep our mouths shut. I added, 'Go to bed, Sammy — I'll come too as soon as I can. I could use an early night!'

The twins were parading to and fro in two identical dresses brought back from Italy at the cost, I was sure, of a great many lire: mindful of

Alex's words, the scene seemed to me strangely sad. After an extended session bedding the girls down, I found Sam even then breathing rebellion: 'He's nice, he's awfully nice! — I told him all about Miss Crocker, he asked what I liked playing best — so I don't see why that bossy old woman — '

'Sam. Hush! *Go to sleep*!'

Eventually, she slept better than I did. There was on my mind the matter of two tapes to be typed urgently, to avoid another possible dose of 'the Rick Corelli charm'.

Very early I was astir, leaving Liz to her fate with the family breakfasts. In the study I sat down to transcribe 'Chapt. 1' on to paper, if it killed me.

It didn't quite. Aware only vaguely of those plaintively wailing gulls somewhere outside — and more mundane sounds from within, people talking, doors shutting — I wrestled with the electronic box of tricks that called itself a typewriter and the semi-foreign voice in my earphones. It was around eleven when the door opened, that same voice said, 'Oh — you're working.'

'Of course. You wanted this done! But this typewriter is a bit of a nightmare! . . . '

Yesterday's first overwhelming impressions flooded back, as I looked round at him. All those publicity photographs here beside me walking and talking . . . perhaps too a tetchy temper, an unfortunate arrogance: but there was more than that apparent to me. Still in his face was that weariness and sadness.

He set down on the desk a small suitcase bulging with something, and asked curtly, 'What's the problem with the typewriter? My Grandmother got hold of it specially.'

'And someone must have been mighty glad to get rid of it!'

He glanced at me with some surprise. Perhaps I should have heeded my own advice to Sam about keeping one's mouth shut. I swept on, 'Apart from that, these notes are — well, not just difficult, don't you really think they're quite a horrendous muddle?'

Whatever his response to that, it sounded colourful. At least he had the grace to swear at me in Italian. I felt bound to apologise, 'Sorry for the plain speaking, but — '

'No need to be sorry. You're right. I don't profess to be a good author.'

It was a rather amazing answer. Almost I blurted out, 'But you're a very, very brilliant pianist, so why waste time trying to write?' — but I hadn't quite the temerity to say that. He was seated by the desk now, looking straight across at me. The nearness of him in the small room, the full gaze of those moody eyes, was utterly disconcerting.

'This is what I'm trying to write about. All this — you see?' He opened the suitcase and spilt out a mass of the contents: a confusion of programmes, folded concert posters, news cuttings — two or three handwritten diaries, disappointingly not written in English.

'This is what my world used to be. There's half a lifetime here. Maybe a whole lifetime.'

'Don't say that, you've a lot of lifetime left!' I remonstrated. 'It all looks really fascinating. I'd love to look through them.'

'Would you? You're very welcome. You think you could produce a better book?'

I shelved the question diplomatically, 'I'm afraid I'm just here to type the thing, not write it as well.'

He said, 'That's a pity,' and he smiled. About the difficult 'artistic temperament' and attendant problems, I had been forewarned. No-one had warned me about the smile. It was like sunlight bursting through stormclouds. Even unexpected twin dimples briefly flickered to life, almost the smile of a lost and pleading child. A smile nearer to being irresistible than any I had ever know . . .

'Er — if I sort these papers out for you,' I struggled to say, 'alphabetic, or date order — would that help?'

'It might. It's kind of you to offer.'

'Er — perhaps,' I plunged again in the need to say something, anything, 'there's a programme of the concert Sam and I tried to see a while ago, that Special Festival week at the Albert Hall? — '

He shook his head doubtfully. I went chattering on. 'Ernst Gausky did the Wagner night — there was a Beethoven programme — and *you* did the Chopin! It was sold right out, I read you had a standing ovation — '

'I did? Who said that?'

'The critic in the *Audience* magazine, Hugo someone . . . He said, 'There are pianists and pianists, tonight we had Riccardo Corelli — his playing lights up the soul!' — I remember reading it out to Sam . . . '

Again, just briefly, his eyes met mine. Now there was no smile. Only a depth of sorrow — and maybe even horror? Indeed, I believed it was that . . .

It had to be this moment when a

sound at the door interrupted us. Alex peered in to address his brother very quietly and civilly.

'Excuse me, Rick. There's a phone call for you, Carl Bergmann from Geneva.'

'I'm busy! Just take the number.'

'No, he's at the airport just catching a plane to London. He wants a word before he leaves — '

Rick gave a long sigh and stood up abruptly, spilling some of the papers on the floor. In the doorway briefly he turned round to me.

'Try to get that work finished today, Rachel — yes?'

The door closed behind him. For a moment there was complete silence, until Alex coughed in obvious embarrassment.

'Sorry. I'm sorry about — '

'I know, the Rick Corelli charm strikes again! Don't worry, I'm developing a hide like a rhino! But — ' I hesitated, groping for words. 'I know he's been ill, he's had troubles. But he seems — very worried, very unhappy. I'm sure he doesn't want to do this book at all. So why has he stopped making his wonderful music and started writing when he *isn't* good at it? — You must know the answer! — '

It seemed to me his mild blue gaze had lost all its light of humour. He was suddenly very busy retrieving the fallen papers, and shut the suitcase with an odd sense of urgency.

'Rick is — a law unto himself. Rachel, you look tired — shall I make you a nice reviving cuppa?'

The answer was no answer at all. But he could solve the mystery if he chose. I was sure he could.

The 'cuppa' didn't happen because of another diversion. Mrs. Nicholson required me to take the twins into Penmoryn, to buy them new school shoes ready for Monday. I demurred, 'I'm supposed to finish this typing. Mr. Corelli won't like it if — '

'A couple of hours won't hurt,' she overturned that briskly. 'Have lunch while you're there. They've been getting under their father's feet this morning . . . just high spirits, of course.'

It was going to be difficult to serve two masters.

Jade and Jenna's bedroom, where I ran them to earth, had colourful clown wallpaper, shelves of expensive-looking books in very mint condition, two white desks and stools. Along the cushioned windowseat a row of dolls, resplendent in the national dress of various countries, stared stonily ahead. They looked as though no small fingers had ever smoothed their hair or cradled them protectively.

The girls were curled up together on one of the beds, their hair awry, their fine dark eyes blotched by recent tears.

'I'll fetch Sam and we're all going shopping,' I invited. 'Five minutes to get ready!'

The two woeful faces became at once masks of defiance.

'We're not buying silly school things! We're *not* going there on Monday!'

'Old Mother Jesmond hates us, she always picks on us! —'

I spared a thought for the unknown School Principal. And yet, how many fresh schools and new faces had figured in their short lives? Alex had surprised me by excusing their bad behaviour, but I was discovering now what he had tried to convey. The silent picture-books, the blank-faced dolls, were devoid of human warmth. The two belligerent little girls were growing up in a vast, puzzling, lonely world.

As they squirmed back from my approach, out of the disarranged bed a small photograph slipped to the floor. I picked it up before they realised.

It had puzzled me a little why there was nowhere at Gull Cliff a likeness of Rick's dead wife — who had so loved this house, had devoted the last months of her life to creating a beautiful home. Now I was looking at a smiling summer snapshot of Christina Corelli . . . a slender young woman, bright-faced, pushing the two little girls on a garden swing. Somewhere back across time, Jade and Jenna had still the chubbiness of babyhood. The three were laughing together. Tina had glorious long hair, dark and loose and free, floating in the sunlight.

A sudden deep sadness ached in my throat. I thought of my own dear mother, of the searing grief of loss, tempered by time, never erasable.

'That's our picture!' A small hand grabbed fiercely at the photograph.

I warned gently, 'Careful! I've a little frame that would just fit, then it won't get spoilt — '

Two heads shook vigorously.

'We can't put it in a frame. 'Cos — we take turns putting it under our pillows. And now you'll tell Great-Gran, then she'll hide it away like all the others!'

'I won't tell her, Jade.'

'*She*'s Jade. I'm Jenna.'

'Sorry. It's a beautiful picture. Keep it safe, and I won't tell anyone,' I promised. For a moment I was tempted to try comforting them in my arms. Instead I said softly, 'I think your Mummy was lovely.'

'Um.' They accepted that with suspicion. 'Bet you're just being nice to us so we'll go to that shoe-shop.'

How could I really fail to forgive them for all their lack of trust in anyone or anything?

* * *

We had lunch in the town. I didn't dispute the twins' choice of chips, lurid green milkshakes and sugary doughnuts. Afterwards, of course, there followed an embarrassing scene in the shoe-shop, where their taste ran on gold sandals or pink 'jellies': I thought Miss Jesmond might not take kindly to either.

Because Alex was busy on some task for his Grandmother, this was the first occasion I didn't have him along for moral support. I missed him:

for his pleasant company as well as his unflappable help with the twins.

It was unfortunate that one of them (now the scratched nose had healed I had big trouble telling them apart) spotted the 'Good Luck' teddy from Dawn stuffed in Sam's pocket. So from then on we had, 'Did lickle diddums bring her teddy-weddy out?' et cetera, plus much sniggering Italian behind Sam's angry back. Definitely, I would have to buy a two-way dictionary.

Back at the house, I shut myself up to work, and perhaps rashly handed Sam a pile of programmes from the suitcase, instructing her, 'Read them all you want but keep them *clean*.' The cloud lifted from her face as she vanished upstairs.

That monkey-puzzle of a 'Chapt.1' was still unfinished when I emerged from the study, stiff of limbs and aching of head, for the evening meal. I heard Sam's voice in the lounge. Amazingly, she was sitting beside Rick on a big sofa, the sandy head and the dark both bent over one of the programmes.

Across the room, Abigail was leafing impatiently through a magazine. The twins sprawled on the floor squabbling over a board-game.

'Yes, Rachel likes the *Consolation*, she plays it a lot at home!' Sam was chattering on, shyness forgotten in rapt excitement. 'Oh, and that one — I can do the first part of that. Till it gets to the *agitato*. Of course, we don't play them like *you* do . . . we've got loads of your recordings, we think they're super! . . . '

He said, 'Grazie.' I saw again those so elusive dimples, just a glimmer.

Sam went glowing with me upstairs to change, and came glowing down to the dining-room in her new apple-green outfit that prettily highlighted her hair.

Around the table this evening there were awkward cross-currents. I guessed Rick and Abigail had had a disagreement: also, his Grandmother was trying none too subtly to get rid of her. 'I'm sure you've other commitments to attend to?' she asked. And. 'How can you cope with the rest of your clients. Abigail, while you're buried away here with us? . . . '

Miss Horton answered with her dazzling blonde smile full in Rick's face and the teasing comment, 'I've only ONE client who matters, haven't I, Ricco? . . . '

Mrs. Nicholson choked, and gulped copious water. Either Liz's apple crumble resembled sawdust, or for once Liz wasn't at fault at all.

Strongly I shared the old lady's satisfaction, a while later, when Abigail mentioned she would soon need to 'pop off to visit Cousin Peg in Bristol.' We were mutually crushed by the careless addition, 'But I'll soon be back with you.'

I noticed that all through that weekend Alex merged himself into the background, busy at a distance in the garden or helping out in the kitchen.

On the Sunday Rick and Abbey actually let the twins pile gleefully in the back of the white convertible for an outing, so the house was quite peaceful. I was able to score a double black line at the foot of 'Chapt. 1'.

But Monday morning wasn't far away. Two blue and white school-dresses were already hanging in the twins' room, complete with little card-board badges lettered JADE and JENNA. I wondered how often it amused them to swap identities. I wondered if anyone ever knew.

The morning dawned grey and misty, as bleak as the girls' faces as they dawdled over breakfast. Mrs. Nicholson was instructing me briskly, 'Don't take the coast road — turn right, left fork, bear right — you can't miss it!'

I felt it was thoughtful of Alex to offer, 'Shall I drive?'

'Well — this once,' his Grandmother conceded. 'But Rachel will do the school runs, you always upset the girls for no reason!'

He said meekly, 'Yes ma'am.'

I was more than glad to be a passive passenger while he pointed out the route — and the twins made the same sort of rude comments on his car as they did on mine.

The Heights was impressive, a spreading grey-stone building backed by green playing fields, with a large modern extension obviously a hall or gymnasium. Other cars were unloading a few shapes and sizes in blue and white. I commented, 'Nice!' — which the twins dismissed with a disgusted, 'Huh!'

'May I suggest.' Alex said mildly, 'hand them over to someone, Rachel, make yourself known. So we've proof they arrived — in case they try hitch-hiking home, they did that once.'

I appreciated the hint. With a twin captive in either hand, I crossed the playground and hailed brightly the duty teacher in the doorway, 'Morning! — Jade and Jenna Corelli, all present and correct. I'm staying at their home and I'll be transporting them from now on.'

'Oh. Will you? Thank you,' she acknowledged, possibly with pity.

In haste I retreated to the car, where Alex fanned himself with a road-map and commented, 'Whew! One morning done, lots more still to go!'

'Why *do* they make such a fuss? It looks a nice place — and there's a notice in the doorway about an 'Annual Music Festival' soon, won't they enjoy that?'

'Not a lot. They're not specially musical. Disgraceful, but true.'

I ventured. 'Was their mother — ? Did Christina — ?'

It surely was reasonable to ask, because anything helping me understand the children in my care couldn't be out of place. But now, as always, there was a certain look on Alex's face, defensive, full of hurt. The tragedy of Tina's death lived on in him. And so how much more, I thought, was it seared into the soul of his brother, of Tina's bereaved husband? . . .

'Tina liked music, she loved to hear Rick play. — Shall we get moving?' Alex said, and started the car.

We didn't hurry. It was a pleasant roundabout drive, as he made diversions to show me 'the scenic route'. We shared admiration of the dramatic Cornish shoreline, the grey and green cliffs, white horses riding on tumbled water, a walled harbour where picturesque boats clustered. We shared as well just ordinary everyday talk, moments of laughter. In the Gull Cliff world, they were precious moments.

Fresh from those, I wasn't too troubled when Mrs. Nicholson's eagle eye watched us cruise in at around eleven. I had already done more than my share of overtime.

But the happy aura of the drive was short lived. Sam ran to find me in a state of sheer panic, dragging me back to the bedroom.

The bundle of concert programmes, placed neatly near her bed overnight, was still there. Several had been scrawled over with a blotchy ballpen. Among those riotous scribbles were accusing signatures: 'Sam T' and 'Sammy' and even 'My name is Sammantha.'

'I didn't do it! Ray. I didn't! You know I *wouldn't* spoil them! — '

I did know. I believed her without question. That rendered no easier the task of explaining this to others who wouldn't.

'It was those twins!' she hissed with a fierceness seldom seen in her. 'I saw them giggling before they went off this morning! When they get back I — I'll — '

'Sammy. I'm so sorry. Try not to worry. I'll sort it out somehow. I know they can be little hooligans, but I think I see *why* they did it — '

'I know why! To get me in trouble with their Daddy — because he was so nice to me last night! And now he'll hate me.' To that piece of amazing perception she added darkly, '*And* they can't spell my name right!'

I tried to calm her down, and bore the violated items away. The only hope was to search for duplicates among the others in the suitcase.

A vain hope, that proved to be. When I went to the study with my incriminating handful, I found Rick was already there, sitting at the desk. He was slumped forward over my erratic typescript of 'Chapt. 1', his head on one arm, his upturned face strangely stricken.

For that instant. I forgot why I was here. I started forward towards him.

'Rick! . . . Rick, are you ill? . . . what can I do? . . . '

It was a relief that he lifted his head. But his black eyes blazed at me.

'Don't . . . *don't* creep up on me! What do you want in here?'

'Well, this is where I work.' I realised, as he sat up, that he had spotted the papers in my hand: certainly it wasn't the best moment for this revelation. 'Yes, I'm sorry about this — you can see what's happened. I don't want to carry tales, but I'm afraid it must be Jade and Jenna's handiwork. Sam certainly wouldn't damage them! — and besides,' I added confusedly, 'her name is spelled wrong . . .'

If I had expected an outpouring of fury, it didn't come. He frowned, but seemed not greatly concerned.

'What do you expect me to do? Aren't you being paid to keep the children in line?' he said harshly. 'Just do your job!'

'I'm trying to! But — this is such a serious matter, wouldn't it be better if you speak to them yourself?'

He made an impatient gesture. 'These are — only pieces of paper! You deal with it, just — leave me alone!'

I looked at him unhappily. In these brief few days it had become plain to me that there was no real bond between him and his motherless children — who readily bragged about his years of fame and their treats and travels, but wept secret tears over their hidden photograph of Christina. How many times in this short while had I seen them run up to him eagerly and receive the same answer, 'Ask your Great-Gran,' or 'Tell me later!'

Almost it seemed he was *afraid* to get close to Jade and Jenna. I thought they needed desperately the love he could give them. I pitied them . . . and deeply I pitied him, a profoundly troubled man — and surely at this moment a very sick one?

I had received my orders, but still I couldn't leave. I was recalling the moment when I tried to soothe the lonely tears of his little girls — and the urge came to me to cradle them in my arms until their grief found solace. It was so very strange that the same longing came to me now with this gifted, difficult, wounded man — to hold him close until his sorrows were comforted, and a great emptiness within me found fulfilment. What sort of compelling madness could that be? I who hardly knew him, who even had hardly liked him — who feared him just a little, who worshipped his genius — who longed to see again that special smile that could light up my heart . . . Against all commonsense and logic, was I really falling in love with him? . . .

I backed away from the desk, aware my face was glowing, that every pulse in my body was racing with this absurd unreal elation. I had to say something. Even if it was just 'Good-bye' — or 'Arrivederci!' . . .

'I — I see you've been looking at the typing. I did my best but — the whole thing really needs — '

What it needed was never given voice. One of those strong slender hands snatched up the file of papers and flung the whole thing across the room — so violently that it upset the jug of flowers in the fireplace with an unholy clatter.

I breathed, 'For heaven's sake! — I didn't say it was *that* bad! . . . '

'What's going on in here?' It was

Mrs. Nicholson's sharp voice and even sharper gaze that made both of us give a huge and guilty start, as she peered suspiciously round the door. 'I thought I heard — ?'

'You did!' Somehow I conjured up a very sickly smile for her as some instinct put words in my mouth — deliberately confused and jumbled words that didn't say much: 'Very sorry about the mess.' and 'such a clumsy accident,' and 'I'll clear it up right away . . .'

'Well, I should hope so.' She surveyed me, from my still burning face to my last summer's sandals. 'I hope you will. Rick, you look exhausted!' she shot at him with a severity no less. 'You're not overworking, are you?'

He shook his head. I chimed in again. 'We're just finishing up here, Mrs. Nicholson. We were just discussing the first chapter.'

She lingered a moment more, and then went on her way upstairs. I looked round at Rick with a taut snatch of laughter.

'Help! There goes my reputation for calm efficiency!'

He said quietly, 'Why did you do that?'

'I — I don't know. I just thought you wouldn't want any questions asked.'

'It was very nice of you, Rachel.'

'My pleasure.' I muttered. I was aware that those dark eyes of his looking straight into mine had magically warmed and softened — until their gaze almost was a caress. I had known they could do that. Somehow I had known . . .

'Of course, I'll explain it wasn't your fault. And — I apologise to you for my stupid behaviour. I hope you can forgive? — '

The softly pleading voice, the smile in his eyes, were churning me up. I breathed, 'Please! — it just took me by surprise, but don't worry about it! Though I can see now where the twins get their tantrums from . . . ' He accepted that without comment, so I stumbled full-tilt into even more plain speaking. 'Can I just ask you — Mr. Corelli — '

'You made it 'Rick' just now. That was nice. Why not stay with that?'

'If — if you say so. Look, please don't think I'm being impertinent — but *why* do this book at all if it bothers you so much?'

'It does bother me,' he agreed. 'And I'm so glad now I have you and your understanding to help me.'

It was no real answer. I said of course I would help. Then the answer did come, unexpected, still enigmatic.

'I was advised to do the book. Take my advice, Rachel — stay away from wise physicians who try out unusual therapies!'

I didn't understand. I said just, 'Oh.' He wasn't smiling now, but the smile was still with me.

It was with me while I went to find a cloth to mop up the fireplace. And now, not that smile alone. It was the way he said 'Rachel'.

3

Whether or not Jade and Jenna were ever called to task about the damaged programmes, I never really knew. I tried to talk to them, and was met by faces of appealing innocence, hints that 'Sammy had them, not us!' The wily pair seemed to go on their way quite unchastened.

As for their 'school run' to and from The Heights, it never failed to cause me major problems. The mornings were worst, when it came to leaving my sister rather smugly behind: they grumbled darkly, 'It's not fair, and there's *laws* about having to go to school! We could tell the police!'

I didn't put them past trying that, or anything else to alarm Sam. The reason their threats failed was her great joy in finding Rick *hadn't* blamed her for the damaged papers.

She followed him around devotedly, she spent hours poring over his music library, she reverently used his piano. With increasing confidence she asked his advice and help.

I hoped she wasn't being a nuisance. It was hard to discourage her hero-worship when my own hidden feelings for him were becoming so much more.

In fact, during the days following those startling moments with him in the study, really I saw him very little. I kept telling myself perhaps that was just as well. I knew he was spending as little time on the book as he could.

Also I was well aware of the undercurrents at Gull Cliff gaining momentum: the atmosphere between the brothers seemed like a tangible presence in the house, smouldering, waiting — at least on Rick's side. Rick whose temper was so dismayingly unstable. Perhaps for light relief he spent quite a time driving around the countryside with Abigail. But even that was evidently not all sweetness and light. I overheard odds and ends of sharp words.

'She wants him to do some concerts in the Autumn,' Alex explained to me. 'Seems like a battle of wills. Interesting!'

Whoever won that battle, come the Autumn I was due back in London. Surely for the sake of the world of music, Abigail *should* succeed — and probably would: she struck me as clever, confident, deeply shrewd. It clearly amused her to start Mrs. Nicholson's outraged eyebrows lifting by appearing in strapless sunwear held up by sheer willpower. There was no doubting her pleasure in being with Rick. That half-possessive, half-teasing 'caro mio' became more frequent . . . as well as the occasional 'Ricco sweetie' or 'Ricky my poppet' . . .

'Most interesting,' Alex summed it all up, as we snatched one of our stolen breaks together on the grass he had just trimmed. 'Depends how soon poor Gran can pack her off to her Cousin Peg in Bristol. Or maybe — if Abbey can stand large doses of the 'RCC' . . . ?'

It was our private abbreviation of the 'Rick Corelli charm'. I laughed at it now rather self-consciously. But we did laugh together quite a lot. At Gull Cliff it was necessary to laugh with someone.

Though there was a proviso about that too. I knew I mustn't delve into Corelli family history, more than Alex had already told me. 'Every respectable family has a skeleton in its cupboard,' he said one day, 'and in this family, I'm it. Say no more!'

His gentle laugh, this one time, didn't ring true.

It was on Friday evening, with the twins celebrating the end of the school week, that two separate phone calls disrupted whatever pattern life at the big house was developing. The first came from Abigail's cousin, who evidently cared for an aged Grandpa. I heard Abbey mutter a feeling 'Damn!'

and then promise impatiently, 'All right, Peg, tell him I'll be there for his birthday — I'll come tomorrow!'

Mrs. Nicholson's undisguised satisfaction didn't last long. The second call was for me: 'Mrs. Guthrie here from The Willows — sorry to ring you so late, Miss Thornton — '

Suddenly I was chilled through. I breathed, 'My father?'

'Don't be alarmed. He had a little fall this evening. Not too serious — but he does seem quite confused. He keeps asking whether you're back from your holidays.'

'Tell him I'm on my way! I could travel overnight if you think — ?'

She didn't feel that frantic haste was needed. He was safely in bed with a mild sedative, he had suffered bruising and shock. She had spoken to Mrs. Marshall, who would visit him early tomorrow. But of course, if I were able to travel back to London it would help.

In the big beautiful sitting-room, with a fresh sea breeze stirring the curtains,

I never doubted Mrs. Nicholson's instant response: 'Of course you must go, Rachel! Make a nice early start tomorrow.'

Alex offered in his quiet way. 'Would it help if I drive you?'

He was sitting by his Grandmother with a chess table beside them, and she had been tut-tutting reflectively. A while back he had told me, 'She taught me when I was a little kid — she just tells a couple of her pawns, 'Don't stand skulking there, get out and win the game!' — and they do.' I wondered whether his clever accountant's mind ever deliberately allowed her to win.

Still muzzy-headed with shock. I was trying to make rapid calculations. If I travelled by car, it would mean more car-sickness misery for Sam: or, could we just drive to connect up with a train? Or maybe she might stay on here a short while until either I returned or made more definite arrangements? . . .

'I'll drive you, if you want,' Alex suggested again.

'Would you? Oh, that would be wonderful — '

Before I could finish pouncing on that offer, it was snatched away from me. Rick said abruptly, 'I've some business in London. Rachel can come with me.'

I looked rather helplessly from one brother to the other. Alex made a very expressive face in a rare show of displeasure.

'Oh. Well, dear me,' Mrs. Nicholson demurred, which was rare in her as well. 'Rick, are you sure you ought to rush off again? What sort of business? — '

'People to see. My accountant for one. Is there any objection to that?'

She didn't pursue the question. Not one single person cared to mention that one of that profession was available in this same room, just being systematically check-mated.

It was settled that my sister would remain here in Cornwall for the present. I escaped upstairs to pile some bits and pieces into a bag. My anxiety for my father, despite Mrs. Guthrie's practised reassurances, was a heavy weight within me. But as well, nameless excitement was stirring all through a long restless night — because of the time ahead with Rick, he and I together, away from the haunted walls and watching eyes of Gull Cliff.

Nor was that uncontrollable thrill made less by an odd moment with Mrs. Nicholson just before leaving, as she pulled me confidentially into the study. She had known, she said, Rick intended a London visit shortly. She had supposed he would go with Abigail. Although of course the circumstances regarding my father were unfortunate, she was glad he was going with me.

I blinked at her and said, 'You are?'

'Certainly! You're a dependable young lady — usually. You've got your head screwed on, my dear.' Coming from her, it was an amazing compliment. She swept on, 'I hope you'll keep an eye out for Rick. He's a wilful boy — when he was ill he was the world's worst patient! . . . he does still get over-tired easily, you see . . . '

I promised to do the best I was able. It was hard to believe she was actually asking me to 'look after' her grandson — even to see him safely back again?

To my huge relief. Sam wasn't too upset at being left behind, especially as she had permission to use the piano. She gave me a note for Pa, written in her careful hand, and I dished out some money and promised Alex would help her buy him a present to send on. I knew, without asking, Alex would help.

While the twins waved indifferently. Sam did shed some tears at the moment of departure. As she stood by the door, Mrs. Nicholson so far softened as to put an arm round her. Doubtless no moping would be allowed when we were gone.

At the last moment Abbey appeared, fresh from the shower in a snow-white bathrobe, to plant a very public kiss on Rick's cheek. She looked, perhaps understandably, none too pleased at the way things had worked out.

Alex bade me a quiet farewell last of all: 'Ring soon, Rachel. We'll take good care of Sam. Mind you take as much time there as you need.'

Lightly, warmly, he squeezed my arm. I whispered, 'Thank you,' and at this moment tears blurred my eyes too as I glanced back at the house.

He shut the car door, and spoke to his brother, very quietly.

'Take it easy, Rick. And — look after her.'

Whatever there was between the two of them, Rick could have answered that. But he didn't answer.

The powerful engine sparked to life, tyres scrunched the gravel. I couldn't quite bring myself to look back again.

* * *

'Aunt Doreen! — hallo? . . . yes, it's Rachel! Have you heard today — ?'

Crammed into a phone booth at a cafeteria-cum-service station, I listened to her voice across the miles. She had more than 'heard', she had just returned from seeing Pa. He was 'a little poorly.' He was still asking for me and for Sam.

'I'll be home this evening for sure.' I promised. 'Not Sammy, she's staying at the house for now. But we're making good progress, this car certainly moves! — '

'Which car? Who's *we*?' my Aunt understandably wanted to know.

'I'm with Rick. Mr. Corelli. He had to go to London anyway, so . . . '

It took quite a lot to disconcert Mrs. Marshall. But she almost stuttered and stammered, 'Goodness gracious, Rachel. WHY didn't you let me know before? — Greg has his machinery brochures scattered everywhere! — and there's nothing to eat! — '

'Rick won't care. He really won't.'

'Well. I care! All right then, I'll get busy here. We'll see you later.'

I imagined her spending the day vacuuming up every minutest speck of dust, sending Greg to the supermarket with a list pages long.

Back in the cafe, Rick was still sitting in solitude in the corner. There was an aroma of cooked food, a hum of chatter from the other tables. His sunglasses and keys lay beside our two empty coffee cups. He asked me quietly how my father was today.

'Doreen didn't say much. But he's still asking for me. When you've had a rest. I'm ready to go.'

'You drive.' He nudged the car keys across to me.

'Drive your car? Are you sure? I'm just used to my little old banger — '

'A car is a car,' he said indisputably. 'Si?'

I muttered, 'Si!' wholly unconvinced.

Outside, among the regiments of other parked vehicles reflecting the sun, ours awaited us magnificiently. I blinked at it.

'Come on. You're not afraid of a

machine. It can't be worse than that typewriter you're always swearing at.'

He was teasing me. For the first time he was. His black eyes were playful, maybe even indulgent? . . . If he looked at me like that, I could have driven a tank.

Until now, it had been an uneventful journey: he drove fast and easily, while I sat thinking about Pa, longing to arrive — and yet treasuring each of these fairytale moments. To sit close beside Rick and watch his face, watch those hands that had brought packed concert halls to their feet . . . if our mission weren't sickness and distress I could have sat there endlessly, he and I in this enchanted speeding world.

It was a little different when I steered out into the flow of traffic. I exclaimed, 'Oh, this is so — enormous! And *alive*! I'm really not sure I can — '

'I suppose you did pass your test?'

'Test? What test?' I laughed nervously.

It was then that there came suddenly to my mind the memory of his arrival at Gull Cliff, of Abbey sitting casually at this same wheel. No, I wasn't going to be worsted by Miss Horton!

So we went on our way. Maybe we weren't making such good time. We were getting there.

Rick had found a concert on the radio. I manoeuvred through roadworks and round-abouts to soaring Wagner . . . and then the voice of some presenter announced, 'Now for a complete change, an example of a true virtuoso of the piano . . . this is Chopin's First Ballade interpreted by Riccardo Corelli in his very special way . . . unfortunately of late we haven't heard him in live performance, but I'm delighted to have picked up a whisper that he'll make an autumn tour this year. I know we'll all look forward to that . . .'

The music flooded the car, and flooded my heart.

For an instant I glanced at the man beside me, sitting still and silent: for me this music was sheerest beauty — and for him plainly a nightmare most hideous. There wasn't pain alone in his face. I believed there was something like stark horror.

I whispered, 'I'm sorry — I'll turn it off — '

'Leave it, if you want.'

I didn't leave it. Suddenly all the glory was gone, there were just the sounds of the road.

'Rick, what is it? — that stupid man talking about a tour? I suppose Abigail's been jumping the gun, drumming up publicity! — just *don't* let her force you into anything if you're not ready! For her it's just good business! — but for you — '

'For me? What for me?'

'I don't know. How can I know! Except I'm sure you're hurting very much . . . and — and I want to help if I can . . . '

'Why should you bother?'

I could find no answer. Not for him, not for myself.

He leant his head back wearily,

turning away from me. After a while I realised he was actually sleeping. The quick glances I stole showed me his face strangely youthful, totally at peace.

So here was I, Rachel Thornton, steering this palace on wheels unattended across the counties of Southern England — with a passenger of international fame slumbering beside me. More than ever this unreal journey was hard to believe. Hard to believe the close reality of the Jekyll-and-Hyde man so changeful, so hard to reach — in his contradictory moods so harsh, so winning, so vulnerable, so appealing . . .

It was some time later when I left the road for a restaurant car-park, because I was badly in need of a reviving drink and a pause for breath. Struggling into a narrow parking space I prompted, 'Rick, are you awake? I'd just like to stop a while . . . '

'Where are we?' He blinked round him. 'You've come all this way? . . . I'm very sorry. Please forgive.

I just — haven't slept since I came to the house . . . '

Of course, because Gull Cliff, for all its beauty, was haunted. For him it was. It was Tina's beloved home that she hadn't lived to see completed.

Together, his hand gently and penitently holding my arm, we went inside. We sat at a window table overlooking a children's play area with a huge absurd purple dragon. He insisted on buying me a meal I could scarcely swallow. Somehow then I started chattering — because now I was worrying about Pa, about Sam — and even, if I needed to remain long in London, what would happen to the Corelli Memoirs.

When I mentioned that, Rick muttered in sotto voce Italian what was certainly an imprecation on books in general and his book in particular. Sam would be all right for a few days, he promised. She had permission to use the sacred piano — and he had made sure to repeat the permission to his Grandmother.

'Your sister has some talent,' he said

seriously. 'No confidence at all — but a real adoration for music. It shines from her like a bright light.'

'I know. You're not suggesting she'll grow up to be a concert pianist too?'

'No, I'm not. I wouldn't wish that fate on her! But she might study seriously, have you thought of doing something about that? Possibly in years ahead she could teach? . . . Aren't you eating that cherry pie? Do you mind if I do?'

I said, 'Be my guest.' Little by little I was discovering, now we were well away from Cornwall, from those four walls and the sound of a breaking sea, that he was changing before my eyes. If the house indeed were haunted, so too was the man.

Now, it was all left behind us . . . and he asked me with warmth and sympathy about the difficult family responsibilities I had shouldered over the years. He said Sam did me great credit, he was sorry if Jade and Jenna hadn't made her welcome. I found myself burbling on, explaining Sam's problems in making friends — in feeling herself an unwanted ugly duckling in a huge unfriendly pond.

'That was really why I answered your Gran's advert, to shake Sam up and change her horizons! But I don't know if it's going to work.'

'We'll try very hard to make it work.' He leant towards me across the table, his eyes looking straight into mine. 'Perhaps I haven't helped you by encouraging her with the music — '

'Oh, yes you have! She's so thrilled that you don't look on her as just a nuisance. It's got to give her ego a big lift! And — I'm very grateful . . . '

I trailed off there. Irrelevantly, painfully, I thought that poor Christina would have sat as I was sitting, listening to this voice, enthralled by these changeful eyes — by the soul looking out of them that could soar to the loftiest heights, sink back to the blackest depths. Back across time, she would have listened and watched — and loved him, and loved him . . .

He said softly, 'Whatever the reason you came to Gull Cliff, I'm glad you came, Rachel.'

Again, once again, the unforgettable way he said my name.

We were ready to leave. I followed him between the tables, the passing travellers eating and drinking and talking, the everyday world still going on. In the doorway an earnest little elderly lady — she was faintly reminiscent of Miss Crocker — made a sudden dive as though finally plucking up courage.

'Excuse me — do excuse me! — but *aren't* you Riccardo Corelli? . . . Oh, I knew it was you! I've heard you play *so* many times! . . . '

He paused to talk to her, to sign an autograph. He smiled at her. I wondered if she would carry the smile away with her to treasure far more than the flourishy 'best wishes' on an old envelope.

Back in the car, it was some relief to

be again a mere passenger as we bowled on towards London. The compact discs he slotted in brought us a feast of impassioned Puccini, not even a ghost of a piano.

Caught up in the spreading tentacles of suburban London, we stopped for petrol. The final few miles I drove again. Beside the splash of green that was the Common we queued in lines of big red buses, grubby lorries, weaving cars. Then a maze of familiar turnings led to the familiar bricked terraces of Bannister Close with their small bright gardens. I couldn't help hoping our neighbours were watching behind their curtains.

Certainly Doreen Marshall must have been. She hurried out while I was making an embarrassing hash of parking.

'Well, goodness alive, child! — '

'Whew! Just made it! . . . Hallo, Aunt Doreen — how's Pa?'

'He's doing all right. A little better. He'll be really pleased to see you, just come in a moment and we'll have time to get round to The Willows.' Never one to stand on ceremony, she was surveying my companion with open curiosity. 'How do you do, Mr. Corelli? — Nice to meet you! Please come inside . . . '

As she bustled him into the house. Greg appeared from the back garden, his broad-shouldered six-feet-plus seeming suddenly to dwarf the visitor.

'Do please sit down, make yourself at home,' Doreen was inviting. 'I hope you'll excuse the muddle in here.'

There wasn't a shadow of a muddle. The room looked more pristine than I had ever known it.

I sat down close beside Rick at the table, which of course was resplendent with the best china and a jug of pure white marguerites — their stems probably trimmed to an exact fraction of an inch.

After one sip of tea I whispered, 'Rick! — can you believe, *not* Earl Grey!'

His eyes and mine exchanged a private smile.

It was only a brief session in this so familiar room because The Willows kept very early hours. The clock was ticking on, the car Greg had hired for his stay waited outside. I was keenly aware of Doreen's sharp gaze, well rivalling Mrs. Nicholson's, noting both the familiar confidential 'Rick' and the private joke. It didn't matter much.

Rick said little, answering pleasantly and patiently what she said to him. No, it was no trouble to escort me home. Yes, it was quite a journey. No, the kind offer of a room here wasn't needed, he was staying with a friend at Wimbledon.

'But you'll come here to lunch tomorrow? — please?' I insisted.

'If you want. If it's no trouble to anyone. Gracie. Thank you.'

'Our pleasure!' Doreen said briskly. 'The least we can do, when you've been so very helpful to my niece! We'll see you around midday, then.'

We parted company out on the pavement, three into one car, one into the other. At the last moment I ran to fetch from it a cardigan left on the back seat.

'I hope you find your father much better.' Rick was writing down a telephone number in those flourishy characters that had delighted the old lady in the cafe: I wondered suddenly, should I ask Miss Crocker to lunch tomorrow too? . . . 'If you need me, Rachel, I'll be here. Just ring me. Promise?'

I whispered, 'I promise. Thank you. Thank you for everything . . . '

As I took the paper, our hands touched. For one moment mine was held fast in his. That was all, no more words. I needed none. The white shape I had unbelievably driven across so many miles slid away down the street.

'Well!' Beside me in Greg's car, as we followed on, my Aunt coughed. 'So that's the great man. Nice looking, of course — in his way. You seem to get on extremely well with him. Rachel, if I may say so.'

'Oh, he — he's being very kind to me today,' I said lamely.

'You mean he isn't always kind to you?'

'He does have his moods. Quite a temper. A throwing things kind of temper!'

In Doreen's world, people behaved themselves. If they didn't, they were made to — like the young Marshall sons she had turned into highly respectable citizens. She gave a disapproving grunt.

'What people call artistic temperament, I suppose. I don't hold with that rubbish! Plus there's the Latin blood, of course . . .'

Her tone of voice made that second accusation sound like a noxious disease.

It didn't matter. I clung to the scrap of paper folded small in my hand. If, please heaven, I would very soon find my father better . . . and if, back at St. Denna, Sam wasn't worrying too much . . . then all the world suddenly was a transcending golden glory of sunshine.

* * *

I sat at my father's bedside that evening, holding his hand, saying very little. In the morning, I found him out of bed and in his wheelchair, huddled in a dressing-gown suddenly too large for him. I moved him out to a corner of the pleasant patio beside a planted container of violas. Other residents spoke to him pleasantly. Mrs. Guthrie buttonholed me to discuss the aftermath of the fall — 'He seems to be settling down — but it's certainly a good thing you could come, he's much brighter today . . . '

I was just thinking of returning home for the 'lunch party' when one of the care assistants ushered another visitor out to the patio. As I looked across at Rick, was it too absurd to feel that the tempered English sunlight had become a tropical blaze, the pale violas were vivid orchids? Would I ever get used to that happening? Would I ever really believe the reason why it happened? . . .

Rick had obtained from somewhere a beautiful basket of fruit for my father, huge black grapes, pears, cherries. He shook hands. I explained shakily, 'Pa, this is the man I'm working for — remember I told you, in Cornwall, and Sammy is there with his family? — '

I wasn't sure how much he understood. As well, suddenly I wondered whether these surroundings awakened painful memories for Rick of his own illness, of which I knew so little?

Outside I had intended a bus ride back. Instead, there was the white car. He explained to me, he had arrived too early for lunch, Mrs. Marshall had told him where I was.

'It was really nice of you to come for me. I'm so glad Pa met you! — it'll make it all more real to him. Oh, and I rang Gull Cliff and everything's fine, I spoke to Sam and Mrs. Nicholson,' I chattered on. 'And no Earl Grey was poured down the phone line! — I think I'm getting withdrawal symptoms!'

He smiled round at me, the twin dimples deepening. He seemed to me very subdued today. I wondered about the 'friend' he was staying with at Wimbledon and where they had met. I didn't choose to consider if the *him* could be a *her*? . . .

Surely he wasn't missing the presence of Abigail Horton — who had planted on him that public kiss yesterday, who was so free with her 'caro mios'. Suddenly fierce defiance bristled. For the rest of our stay in London and the long drive back, it wouldn't be my fault if he did miss her!

When we arrived at the house, it was nice to find little Miss Crocker perched on a chair in a state of awed reverence, her fluffy grey hair smoothed down, her faded blue eyes quite starry. She had just found my message on her answerphone and hurried straight round. I made sure she sat beside Rick at the table. Of course, that led to long discussions on Claudette Martine's interpretation of the Liszt, or whether Maestro Mandelli conducted the Beethoven as though he had a train to catch.

'I did hear you play that Concerto, er — er — Rick,' she breathed. (I had insisted she called him that, I thought it would be the thrill of her life.) 'In Birmingham, I was staying with my sister Lucy . . . and the First Violin had a nose-bleed, you passed him over a handkerchief. Lucy and I always remember that! . . . '

I saw him frowning, his face strangely ageing and darkening. Quickly I answered for him, 'The act of a true Good Samaritan, I wish I'd seen that too!'

Aunt Doreen was also frowning. It was no wonder with so little heed being paid to her home cooking.

Miss Crocker glowed as I had seen

Sam glow before her. While we still dallied over coffee, another guest arrived: Dawn, who I had phoned earlier, who was briefly truanting from Robbie's mother's birthday 'do'.

The coffee was circulating in the crowded sitting-room. Facing us was the well-worn upright piano. In the other corner, where my modest hi-fi system and recordings lived, one had been balanced on the shelf so it stood out: '*Corelli Plays Favourite Classics*'. Perhaps a little obvious of Doreen.

Dawn, her usual bubbly self-confident self, didn't talk about music. Perched on the arm of the settee beside Rick, she recalled the holiday she and Robbie had in Italy: 'Lake Como . . . the colours were so gorgeous . . . Robbie took some super slides of Milan Cathedral . . .'

Again Rick's face was stern, his answers brief in his softly accented voice — and again, like the nose-bleed reference, I had an unexplained instinct to 'rescue' him. I was being silly, of course. Dawn clearly noticed nothing amiss, sailing on to the question one of us dared even approach.

'Well, here we are, a captive audience! And by a lucky chance here's a piano! So can I ask a big favour before I rush off? — something to tell my children and my grandchildren? — '

I wanted to shout at her, 'Don't ask him! — he won't — or he *can't*? . . . ' Instead I blurted out, 'Dawn, it'll cost you! Performance fees *plus* my commission!'

'Oh. Then I'll defer it till my next pay cheque.' She laughed, gathering up her bag. 'Anyway, I must fly. Can't afford to get in Mum-in-Law's black books!'

She bade everyone a cheery farewell, and I went with her to the front door. In the porch she whispered, 'Well, some people have all the luck! I thought I found you an employer, not a walking dreamboat!'

'He isn't always,' I said unconvincingly.

'You've got to make allowances for artistic genius. Look, you come and work in the Employment Bureau and I'll work for your mean and moody and altogether gorgeous Riccardo — any day!'

Of course, she commented too on the white car gleaming away expensively at the kerb. Shiny cars, beautiful seaside houses, after all didn't count for so much. I was coming to realise that in Rick's life they didn't.

Dawn's departure was the signal for the 'party' breaking up. Miss Crocker faded away, probably for aspirins and a lie-down. Rick left for Wimbledon, thanking Doreen for her hospitality — and thanking me, with the warmth of his sad dark gaze, for whatever I had done for him. Soon after, I went with the Marshalls back to The Willows.

It was quite late in the evening, with Greg tending the garden and Doreen busy in the kitchen, that I dialled Rick's scribbled number. I had to speak to him. On the pretext of reporting on Pa — on any pretext — I had to.

There was an answerphone. A man's

thickly accented voice greeted me.

'Dr. Carl Bergmann is not home at present. Please leave your number. I will call. If the matter is urgent please ring . . . '

I didn't wait for that. However urgent my case, it wasn't medical aid I needed.

'Rachel?' Doreen called to me. 'I want to say something to you!'

She regarded me sharply over the half-prepared supper.

'Do you know what amnesia is?'

'Do I know — ' I echoed blankly. 'Yes! Loss of memory. Caused through an injury or a bad shock?'

'Exactly. And you know, of course, I was once upon a time a nurse? I had specialised training?'

I nodded. I watched her slice a tomato. 'Are you talking about Pa. or — '

'Not your father. I'm not at all happy about this man you're working for. I was watching him.'

'I know you were watching him!

And it's a crazy idea.' I burst out, 'for goodness sake, isn't he writing his memoirs? Isn't that why I'm there at St. Denna?'

'But you said he was having a lot of trouble with the writing?'

'Ye-es.' I conceded. 'A lot.'

'Does he rely on old diaries, photos, programmes?'

'Ye-es. All the time. But that doesn't mean . . . ' I stopped short there. 'He did advise me once to 'avoid physicians who try out strange therapies'. But — '

'Exactly!' she said again. 'Rachel, we all know he's a brilliant man. I believe he's also a very troubled man. It could be some intermittent problem that comes and goes — but something's not right. I had the feeling there's something in his mind that he daren't face up to. So he may be half-consciously blocking it out. Well, that's my opinion, take it or leave it!'

I wasn't at all inclined to accept her highflown theory. I challenged, 'His wife Christina died very suddenly, surely he's entitled to be upset about that! And his children are running wild, they're really very forlorn and mixed up too — that must worry him as well. Then there's some horrendous quarrel he had with Alex. It's quite frightening, they're more like arch enemies than brothers — '

'Tell me about Alex. You haven't said much about him.'

'He's older than Rick. He's very tall. He's — nice.' I reflected. 'Quiet and kind and gentle. And funny. He's been wonderful to me, we've had some good times.'

'Hm!' She planted the last sandwich on the plate. 'And how does your sister cope with all this?'

'Sammy? Oh, not so well at first — but she's settling down. And she adores Rick!'

She received that with another 'Him. Well, you know I always speak my mind. If you're still going to work at this Cliff House place — '

'Gull Cliff. Of course I am!'

'Then will you take a word of advice? I daresay, being tied up with your father and Sammy, you haven't had a lot to do with young men . . . '

I bristled anew, 'I'm not a child. I've had my moments!' Not very exciting moments, nor very recent. Moments, nevertheless.

Doreen ploughed on undeterred. 'When you go back, Rachel — do your work, enjoy your seaside. But otherwise, *leave well alone*. You're a sensible girl. Stay sensible and keep your feet on the ground! . . . Are we ready for this supper now?'

'I'll carry it through.' I said soberly.

The orderly tray would certainly make one of Liz's efforts look like an explosion in a bakery. Alex's amused blue eyes weren't there to share that passing thought. Nor the impenetrable depths of Rick's eyes that had come to haunt my waking and my sleeping.

It occurred to me as well, I hadn't got round to telling Doreen that Rick's host in Wimbledon was a *Dr.* Carl

Bergmann, lately flown in from Geneva, Switzerland. But after all, did she really need to know?

* * *

The telephone lines were buzzing again early in the morning. This time, the first call didn't originate with me. It came from a pay-phone, with an assortment of background noise.

'Rachel? — Alex! . . . Look. I've got to be quick. We had some trouble last night. I'm in Penmoryn, at the Hospital — '

I breathed, 'Sammy?' These telephone shocks were becoming altogether too much.

'No, Sam's fine — back at the house with Liz and the twins. It's Gran. She fell on the stairs. It was — a bad fall . . . '

'I'm so sorry. That's awful. How bad is it? — can you tell me — ?'

He scarcely could. It was quite hard to follow his explanations.

'Bad enough. Oh, the twins were 'haunting' Sam — dressed up in white sheets as that wretched Lady of St. Denna — and Sam panicked and screamed and ran — and Gran was just coming up to investigate and they collided head-on on the stairs . . . oh, you'll hear all the story later. It was all so silly, so unnecessary! . . . Sam wasn't hurt at all, but very shocked and upset. They're putting Gran's leg in plaster, they say it will be all right, but — she's not very young, you see . . . '

The Alex I had often deemed 'unflappable' sounded breathless, and there was a break in his voice. I knew the depths of his attachment to the old lady, who had cared for him devotedly through his childhood years. Whenever he made comments about her undoubted quirks of character, always it was with amused indulgence, never unkindness.

'Alex, listen. Listen to me! She's very strong, isn't she?' I insisted. 'She has enormous willpower! She'll be all right, she'll soon be ordering everyone around in the hospital . . .'

He didn't answer that. There was no trace of his usual easy-going manner.

'Will you do something for me, Rachel? I suppose you're in touch with my brother? — will you please tell him what's happened? If I ring him he'll just put the phone down on me.'

'He wouldn't! — would he? . . . All right. I'll ring right away,' I promised. 'We'll come straight back to Gull Cliff! I know that's what he'll want to do.'

I spoke a few moments more: Pa was much better, I would say a quick goodbye this morning and hopefully visit him another weekend when this new crisis was over. I kept telling Alex not to worry, to get some rest — I guessed he had been up all night. It was strange to be calming and advising the Alex Corelli who had been always such a tower of strength to me.

After that, I dialled the Wimbledon number. This time there was the gutteral voice of Dr. Bergmann in person. Then there was Rick's voice, and I poured out my story.

'I can be ready by eleven, I'm calling in to see Pa first . . . '

'I'll pick you up. Rachel, if you're sure you want to go back today?'

'Of course I'm going back! Can you imagine Liz coping with everything at the house? And — poor Alex sounded really tired and worried. Quite exhausted.'

'Did he?' Rick said curtly — which ended that conversation.

He did collect me on the dot of eleven. The morning was all a frantic rush, but I managed a few private moments with Mrs. Guthrie at The Willows. Finally, I was watching from the sitting-room as Rick's car slid to a halt at the gate.

Greg encircled me with a warm strong arm and told me to look after myself. Doreen added to one of her brief businesslike embraces a final word, '*Don't* forget what I said to you!'

'Common-sense,' she had said. 'Feet on the ground,' she had said. I promised I wouldn't forget. Then I was hurrying out to the pavement — and the nearness of Rick.

Of all my travels over this increasingly familiar London/Cornwall route, today's was the quickest: more rapid than our joint driving venture, though I did take over for a couple of minor spells. We listened to some orchestral tapes. We shared a hasty meal, the two of us uncannily alone among chattering, munching, quaffing humanity.

Again, like last time, if it were not for the circumstances I could have wished this journey to go on and on.

It was a mild and beautiful summer evening when we cruised at last up the steep approaches to Gull Cliff. Before our wheels stopped, I heard shrilly raised children's voices. An untidy, quite frantic looking Liz flew out to us, almost dragging us inside.

'Am I glad you're back! It's been a nightmare here! Look, I know I'm supposed to do the cooking and be general dogsbody — I *never* came here to be nanny to those little devils of kids! — '

'It's all right, Liz,' I tried to soothe her. 'We're back now. Calm down!'

Rick asked abruptly, 'Where are the little devils of kids?'

'Sorry, Mr. Corelli,' she muttered. 'But they are, when they want to be! They're supposed to be in bed early for being naughty — but it sounds like they're playing at earthquakes up there! — '

'Where's Alex?' I asked. 'Alex would have helped you with them!'

'He's still at the Hospital, he's been there most of the day. Oh, Mrs. Nicholson's drinking now and talking, he said when he last rang — but she won't be home for a while yet. She was BAD last night, I can tell you. She bumped down all those stairs. She hit the bannister, there was gallons of blood everywhere . . .'

I was sorry for Liz, but she could

have shown more tact. She chattered on dramatically all the way up the fateful staircase.

It was a new shock to find Sam barricaded in our bedroom: I had wondered why she hadn't run out to meet me. Now, at the sound of my voice, she dismantled various chairs and suitcases in a noisy jumble and collapsed into my arms. I held her close, my face against the bright hair escaping from a straggly plait.

'I didn't push her downstairs!' she burst out. 'They keep saying I pushed her! — '

I breathed, 'Of course you didn't! Sammy, who says you did?'

'The twins — and maybe Liz too — they all think I did! Oh, I — I know I've said things about her being bossy and grumpy, but . . . '

I held her tightly, rocking her like a young child. 'It was an accident. Of course it was.'

She wasn't easily soothed, still shaking and clinging to me. And nor in the room down the landing did Rick seem to be having much success with Jade and Jenna: after a few moments, still holding tightly to Sam's hand, I went to see what was happening. Both girls were half-dressed and tempestuously sobbing. Jade was face down on her bed. Jenna was protesting, 'It was just a *joke*! — only Sam was such a scaredy-cat! — and if Great-Gran gets dead it'll be *her* fault! — '

As she bounced on to her own bed, I was horrified to see that photograph of Christina slide half-out from under the pillow. Of course, I knew what it was. From where her father stood across the room it would be less obvious.

'Jenna, that's enough,' I stopped her short. 'No-one's going to be dead! But it was a very unkind trick you played, wasn't it?'

'It was a joke!' she flared at me. 'Just a joke with a silly old sheet! — '

In the midst of this, a car was drawing up outside. There were light steps on the stairs. I looked round at Alex in the doorway, his ice-blue eyes bereft of all their gentle laughter, his high sunburnt forehead creased in unfamiliar lines.

I greeted him, 'Hallo!' — as no-one else seemed inclined to do so. 'How is she tonight?'

'She's sleeping now. She's very shaken up. I've never seen her look like she looks . . . ' He turned suddenly to his brother face to face. 'I hope you've told your children exactly what their behaviour has done to a very old lady! I hope you realise she's given them more time and care than *you* ever troubled to give them all their lives! . . . No, I'm not finished, don't you walk away from me! . . . '

Quite belligerently he barred Rick's way. I hadn't ever seen this side of Alex. I hadn't ever suspected it existed.

'You always had time to travel around like a king, didn't you? — bowing to your audiences, pumping up your own ego — or playing the wounded hero and wallowing in self-pity! When did you ever stop to think about how your family were living their lives? How your kids were growing up? Answer me! Or how their — '

He didn't quite say Christina's name. It wasn't really needed. The likeness of her young laughing face lay there for all to see. Her presence at Gull Cliff had never been stronger.

I thought by now Rick would have blazed back in dangerous rage. But he didn't, his dark eyes glazed over with a quiet that was strangely chilling. In that same unnatural calm he spoke to Alex.

'I don't have to listen to this. One more word from you and you're out of this house!'

'Oh yes? That's the easy way, isn't it? Sweep me under the carpet one more time! One day, Riccardo, you're going to find you can't hide from the truth for ever! — '

'Rachel.' Rick turned to me, stonily stern. 'Will you kindly get the children to bed? — or do you intend letting them stay up all night?'

I opened my mouth and shut it again. He did have a rather devastating way of always finding a scapegoat. Far more important was the need to stop Alex carrying his impassioned tirade further.

I caught hold of his arm and hung on. 'Alex, leave it! — please, not now! — '

As I tugged him aside, it was enough to let Rick pass him and stalk straight out of the room. I heard his door shut along the landing. Dubiously I relaxed my grip on Alex's arm — which he could have flung aside anyway.

'Whew! Would you go down and put the kettle on? — we all need a reviver!' I suggested shakily. 'You'd like some hot chocolate, Jade? — Jenna? — '

Jenna snuffled, 'We've cleaned our teeth. Great-Gran says we mustn't ever have anything after that.'

'Never ever,' her sister gave gruff agreement. 'Still. As she's not here . . . '

Alex's face was still alight with anger.

But he didn't object to the errand. While he was gone I managed to get the twins into identical Mickey Mouse nightshirts. Suddenly they looked very small, very vulnerable, both frightened and subdued by those few moments of fierce unrestrained conflict. On Sam's behalf I had felt, until now, that the pair of them deserved major retribution: if this was really a sample of their home life over the years, perhaps you needed to reconsider.

The forbidden treat arrived in steaming mugs, and they sat up to sip it. Almost I wondered if they would reject their Uncle's offering — 'We don't want it if you made it!' They didn't do that.

He said to me quietly, 'Yours is in the kitchen, Ray.'

'I'll be right down!' I promised.

I was sitting on one of the beds, and a silent pale-faced Sam huddled beside me with her own mugful. She was probably far more upset by the disturbance than the twins. Her world had encompassed so much less than theirs.

'Listen to me a minute, girls,' I said gently. 'All of you listen! *No-one* meant to hurt poor Mrs. Nicholson. But she has been hurt quite badly. I think in future everyone must try very hard not to cause her any more trouble. And tomorrow you can spend a while painting 'get-well' cards to take to the Hospital. Will you do that?'

Sam contributed a shaky assent. Jade muttered, 'We don't need to. We've got lots of money to buy nice cards with.'

'But Great-Gran would much rather have ones you made yourselves.'

'Um. Would she? My drawings always come out sort of funny,' she admitted. 'But if you think she'd like that best . . . ' She added a severe reproof to her sister, 'Jen, don't *slurp*! Great-Gran wouldn't like it!'

I left them a few minutes later, bending over each bed to smooth pillows and administer some soothing strokes and pats. I didn't quite go as far as good-night hugs, which they might leap out of bed to avoid.

Or maybe they wouldn't. I thought that Jade — maybe just slightly the more amenable of the two — was tempted to hang on to me for comfort.

Along the landing Sam's tumbled bed needed straightening as well. I promised her, 'I'll be back in a few minutes.' She was already sorting out drawing-paper and felt-tips, pushing her glasses up her nose in businesslike fashion. She confided, 'They're *weird* people here. aren't they?'

I could only agree to that.

Downstairs, Liz had made herself very scarce, and Rick hadn't reappeared. In a way that was a relief, though I was deeply worried for him. Today's journey, all our recent hours of closeness, seemed at this moment totally unreal.

At the kitchen table, surrounded by Liz's accumulation of crumbs and unwashed crockery, Alex was sitting in an unusual attitude of complete weariness. In silence he passed me over a mug.

'Thanks. Alex, should we — ought we to take something to your brother?'

'You can. If you really want to wait on him hand and foot.'

'Oh,' I muttered.

He looked at me then a little shamefacedly over the table, with just a ghost of his pleasant smile. 'Sorry about the circus just now. I didn't mean to flip my lid — I should have waited to talk to him alone. Only — it's Gran, you see. She's — she's all I've got.'

I nodded in understanding sympathy. But he went on just as though I had asked an obvious question.

'Yes, all right, there are all the Italian Corellis!' (Clearly he lumped Rick in with those.) 'But they're not really mine. Gran is mine.'

'I know,' I said softly. 'And she'll get well. She will.'

There was something like a break in his voice. Involuntarily I reached for his hand, in the same support and comfort that many times he had given to me. It closed on mine, and held fast.

'Of course you're right, it'll certainly take more than a few stairs to get the better of Iris Nicholson!' Still there was a reflection of fierce anger and deep abiding pain in those pale clear eyes. I longed to ask him what lay behind that disturbing scene in the bedroom, but I couldn't frame the words: he would tell me, when he wanted to. If ever he did. 'Rachel, I'm sorry, I haven't asked you yet about your father . . . '

It was a good chance to turn the subject. I started describing my visits to The Willows — though it wasn't easy to talk about the weekend without including Rick. I chattered on about Doreen and Greg and Dawn. At length, he asked quietly the question that hung between us.

'And — did Rick behave himself?'

'He was very good to me. He couldn't have been more kind and helpful! He — he took Pa a whole mass of fruit . . . '

'Nice of him.'

My answers weren't what he had wanted to know. I realised that now, with the two mugs cooling unheeded, with his hand still clinging to mine now warm and strong, his eyes searching my face.

He leant closer to me, and I believed he was going to kiss me. In another moment he would have kissed me. It was sad that I couldn't let that happen.

'I'm sorry, but — I promised Sam I wouldn't be long,' I mumbled.

My hand broke free from his.

4

At Gull Cliff, time and events never stood still. In the days after my return there, it seemed they moved faster even than usual.

Alex and Rick called to see their Grandmother at the Penmoryn Hospital — separately: Alex religiously every day, Rick a few times. The three 'get well' cards produced by the children were propped at her bedside when one afternoon I joined Alex's visit. She was obviously under the effects of pain-killers, her face bruised, her eyes dulled, and she didn't seem particularly glad to see me. For Alex there was a list of sharp enquiries, 'Are you keeping out of your brother's way?' . . . 'You're *sure* you're not upsetting Rick? . . . '

Without her hand on the reins organising and peacekeeping, a deterioration in the household was soon apparent. Liz's slapdash efforts in the kitchen were more than once abandoned completely while she dashed out to see her new boyfriend, a Stevie Somebody whose father owned a small Art shop in St. Denna. Once, Liz woke us all up returning at past two in the morning. It fell to Alex and me to remind her she had obligations to fulfil at the house — and the family were entitled to their sleep.

In fact, a great many things fell to Alex and me. The twins creating Bedlam every school morning, all sorts of mundane household chores, had to be attended to by someone. I felt duty bound to keep things in some sort of order ready for Mrs. Nicholson's return.

Alex's help made it possible. He was always there when I needed him, making light of our shared domestic crises. As for continuing his confrontation with Rick, I knew he was carefully avoiding that. Still I was amazed by the scene that made known a new side of Alex Corelli — a man of strong passions beneath that mild pleasant smile.

Between whiles, I continued work on the book, spending hours sorting the source material — mostly when everyone else was in bed. Pushed well back in my thoughts were Aunt Doreen's theories about the state of Rick's mind: of course, she didn't know him, or understand his special world of blinding light and destroying darkness. I knew him so much better.

Abigail Horton duly arrived back, far more hindrance than help: I couldn't argue when Liz christened her 'Lady Muck'. Most of all, it was deeply hurtful to me now whenever she drove off with Rick, or draped herself on the arm of his chair with her long blonde hair drooped over his shoulder to murmur, 'Ricco, shall we go to Tide Point today?' . . . or 'Ricky, sweetie, the Penmoryn Theatre has quite a decent play on this week? . . . '

It clearly annoyed her that Sam still

followed him around like a devoted shadow. I heard her comment sharply, 'That kid should be in school! — how much more time are you going to waste on her?'

On Sam's behalf I boiled. I was quite unprepared for the outrageous methods Abigail used to get her own way.

Friday morning saw her accompanying Rick to the Hospital, in a very decorous high-necked outfit, bearing an offering of blush-pink roses. Friday lunchtime. I answered the phone to hear an unknown voice asking for me.

'Is that Miss Thornton? — ah yes! This is Miss Jesmond. From The Heights.'

My immediate thought was that the twins had burned the place down. But no, they came into this only indirectly.

'About your young sister, Samantha. Just twelve. I believe? . . . Mrs. Nicholson rang me today, and I understand it would be desirable for Samantha to join Jade and Jenna here till the end of this term . . . so when you collect them, Miss Thornton, perhaps you'd come a little early and bring her to see me? . . . '

Momentarily I was struck dumb. I wanted to shout at her, 'Desirable for *whom*?' — that I had given no permission or agreement, that Sam's education was *my* concern!

She was chatting on pleasantly, 'Good, I'll look forward to seeing you both. *So* unfortunate. Mrs. Nicholson's accident! I'm so pleased that she's improving! . . . '

The call was over before I could pull myself together sufficiently to protest. But I soon recovered enough to storm out into the garden, where Rick and Abigail were sitting together. I demanded without ceremony, '*Who* persuaded Mrs. Nicholson to ring that school about Sam without even consulting me? — *or* consulting Sam? She isn't a parcel to be posted off at a moment's notice!'

I hadn't realised Sam was actually within earshot. I might have guessed she wouldn't be far away from Rick.

Abigail gave me the same sort of look she might accord something slimy emerging from the lily-pond.

'No need to get so excited, Rachel. Rick felt your sister distracts him from the literary work he's trying to do — '

'Nothing like as much as *you* distract him!'

She raised beautifully crafted eyebrows to dismiss that intervention.

'If you'll just let me speak? We discussed it with Rick's Gran this morning, and she quite agreed — '

'You mean it was your idea, *you* discussed it!' I flared. 'And poor Mrs. Nicholson isn't in a position to judge, is she? I'd just like to know what business it is of yours to interfere!'

'Rick's welfare is my business,' she countered that smartly. 'And I don't know why you're complaining. Mrs. Nicholson said she'd adjust your salary to cover costs — and Sam will be better off than getting in the way here and falling behind with her schooling! . . . Isn't that right, Ricky?' she appealed to him.

I was acutely disappointed that he just shrugged his shoulders. He gave no opinion, just requesting curtly, 'Would you ladies mind not arguing over my head?'

Though my mind hastily conjured up excuses for him, I believed he *could* have prevented this if he had troubled to do so. I was quite sure he didn't find Sam a nuisance! During those magic hours of our London journeys, hadn't he actually promised any help he could give to solve her special problems?

He got up and vanished into the house, obviously demonstrating that he had better things to do. I told Abigail shortly, 'Well, I'll see Miss Thingy this afternoon — but that doesn't mean Sam will go to the school!'

'Oh, but I don't mind going,' Sam piped up amazingly. 'If Rick really wants me to go. I'll go!'

For the second occasion in a short space of time I was lost for words.

Abigail laughed her lilting laugh.

In a real huff I told Sam. 'If you want to go, all right, you can! — but don't blame me if you don't like it!'

That was how we came to be ushered into the Principal's room later that afternoon. She received us at a mahogany desk surrounded by shelves of books and framed photographs of school groups, beaming young tennis players, tableaux from previous Music Festivals. Miss Jesmond, surprisingly, wasn't large-bosomed and imposing with ropes of pearls: small, quiet of dress and speech, her silver-blonde hair simply cut, she had an engaging smile.

For a few moments she asked Sam about the work she was doing. Although Sam was her painfully shy self, I was surprised by the way she spoke up, her glasses glimmering earnestly across the desk.

'Very good, Samantha,' Miss Jesmond approved. 'Yes, I'm sure you'll fit in nicely. And you're extremely interested in music. Mrs. Nicholson told me?'

'Yes. I — I've been playing Rick's — Mr. Corelli's piano. He lets me. And he helps me a whole lot . . .'

'Well, well.' Miss Jesmond smiled across at me. 'It's not everyone who can have tuition from the likes of Riccardo Corelli! Samantha, if you're starting with us next week, I'll make sure you have some time with Miss Roberts. She's the Head of our Music Department, she'll want to see what you can do! We have our big musical event coming up very soon, you know.'

Sam reacted with a mingling of delight and alarm. I was still quite bemused by her whole attitude. You could almost say she was taking things in her stride?

All the arrangements were duly made. The following morning, deliberately leaving the twins to the mercies of Rick and Abigail. I drove Sam into Penmoryn to buy a sky-blue blazer to receive the school badge, a light-grey summer skirt and a couple of white shirts to be graced by the official tie. The colour scheme suited her, turning her sandy hair red-gold. Still more I was amazed to find her parading before our bedroom mirror in her new regalia.

'Nice,' I conceded grudgingly — and found my camera to take several shots to send home.

The twins naturally did their best to spread alarm and despondency: 'You'll probably have Miss Robbins, she's the *horriblest* teacher there,' and 'They'll most likely put you in Shakespeare House, they always lose *everything*.' They were sure she would be a laugh a minute in the gym and a disaster on the tennis courts.

Sam retorted with spirit. 'Don't care if I am! The Head of Music wants to see me specially. Miss Jesmond said so.'

'That's nice,' Rick said, and touched her shoulder in kindly encouragement. 'Try her with the *Song Without Words*, Sam. We'll go over the ending again this evening, si?'

Sam echoed, 'Si!' and almost purred. Jade and Jenna glowered, their jealousy perhaps understandable.

There were two more major happenings looming. Mrs. Nicholson was coming home — and though she was still scarcely mobile, her all-seeing eyes would search out every sign of neglect in the house, or hint of discord in the family. As well, I learnt that next week her nephew, one Ralph Kingston, would call on us overnight bringing his daughter to stay for a prearranged holiday. In the circumstances, Mr. Kingston had put the visit forward a week so his daughter could 'help out'.

I appealed to Alex for information: 'I suppose you know them? What's she like?'

'Georgie? She's starting Drama School in September, she treats everything like a Greek tragedy. Uncle Ralph is a prosperous businessman — and looks it.' Alex made one of his expressive faces. 'There'll probably be some family gossip — or scandal, with us it's all much the same . . . I can't see Georgie hoovering the stairs for us, but maybe she'll sit with Gran and divert her attention from the dust!'

He smiled at me, but it wasn't his usual smile. Somehow I sensed he was uneasy about the new arrivals. I couldn't quite imagine why.

This was Sunday evening, and the garden was cool and beautiful. Dusk was just merging into darkness, the rose-and-gold sunset had paled. Distinctly there came from below the restless rush and fall of the tide, so that almost I believed I could feel the cold spray on my face. Lights shone out from the big house: in the conservatory Rick and Abigail were sharing the wickerwork sofa and a deep discussion.

Noting that, involuntarily I sighed as I turned back to the house. Alex said, 'Must you rush away?'

'I have to check some typing for Rick. I've been trying to do it all day.'

'Rachel, this is Sunday evening. Can

you forget the typing for five minutes?' I thought he added, low voiced, 'And even manage to forget my brother too? . . . '

Gentle but insistent his hand on my arm drew me down the path. I was aware of my heart starting to race. I sensed what would come next — and I didn't want it to happen, if it must mean Alex being hurt. It mattered very much that he mustn't be hurt . . .

'It's nice out here,' he said quietly.

'It's lovely. Thanks to all your hard work!'

'Oh.' He waved a hand. 'Gran likes things tidy. It's no trouble to root out a few weeds for her.'

There were others here, I thought, who didn't care to take that much trouble. Deliberately I went chattering on about Mrs. Nicholson, how relieved he must be that she was coming home. He agreed a little restively.

'Yes, you were right, you said she'd come through it all. Rachel, I want to say something to you. I suppose this is as good a time and place as any.'

We were sitting on the garden bench where once Liz displayed an outrageous inch of midriff. In the dusk, as he turned to me, those pale, clear, luminous-blue eyes of his shone forth their message like a beacon . . . gentle, tender, loving, wanting.

A few days back he had almost kissed me. This time, it was less simple to do what I had to do.

I whispered shakily, 'Please, Alex . . . please don't spoil what we have. We — we're good friends, aren't we? And — that means a lot to me — '

He didn't answer, except just a sharp intake of breath as though at a stab of pain. More unsteadily still I stumbled on. 'I do care for you a lot — as a very dear friend. Please believe that. But if you want more than that, I can't give it to you. I'm so very sorry, I hope — I hope we can go on being . . . '

My voice broke, and no more words would come. I felt his arm tighten around me.

'It's all right. Don't worry about it. I'll survive. I always survive . . . but you know I love you very much, don't you? If ever you need me. Rachel — if ever you do — I'll be here. Promise you'll remember that?'

I whispered that I would remember. For an instant more he held me close to him. The distant sounds of the sea, the scents of the summer dusk, were all sadness.

Almost, at this moment, I could have surrendered to the tender warmth of the arms that enclosed me. If my heart still were mine to give.

I broke gently away and stumbled back into the house.

* * *

On Monday morning I took three pupils to The Heights. The twins, used to speculating on the fearful penalties awaiting anyone who missed school, had the wind taken out of their sails. In the car they sat in glum silence.

When we arrived, they eyed Sam in her smart new outfit as I handed her over to the teacher on duty — who I had met a few times.

'This is your sister? — well, how nice,' Miss Carstairs beamed. 'I'm really pleased to see you, Samantha! I'm sure you'll be very happy with us.'

I knew Sam was inwardly petrified, but she wasn't letting it show in front of Jade and Jenna. She managed her shy, attractive smile. Miss Carstairs could hardly inspire great alarm as she took Sam under her wing, promising me she would take her inside and get her organised. Perhaps I was looking more upset than Sam was.

So that was that. With my sister installed at The Heights, the next major event would be Mrs. Nicholson's return home tomorrow. I felt it wise to attempt as major a 'spring-clean' at Gull Cliff as we could manage in the time: Liz was roped in for the vacuuming, I scurried around with dusters and polish, Alex filled flower-vases and moved furniture to turn the study into a temporary ground-floor bedroom for the invalid.

I tried not to be awkward with him, but it seemed we spoke very little. If he was avoiding me I couldn't blame him, but it saddened me.

Abigail had some sort of business summons to London the next day, so Rick drove her to catch a main-line train, and would detour to the Hospital to collect his Grandmother. That was his decree, so that was how it was done. I had hoped he might ask me to go along, but he didn't. Certainly he didn't ask Alex.

I was actually out on the 'school-run' when Mrs. Nicholson arrived. I returned home with the girls to find her reclining on a sofa in the big sitting-room, a tray of Liz's dubious refreshments beside her. I was a little shocked by her drawn face.

But her eyes were sharp, her voice was clear. She greeted me. 'Well, Rachel, here I am, safe and sound, all in one piece!'

'It's really nice to have you home.' I said sincerely. 'We've all missed you very much! — haven't we?' I prompted the twins with a nudge.

They chorused dutifully, 'Nice to have you home, Great-Gran. Hope you're feeling better, Great-Gran.'

It was Sam who actually approached the sofa to extend a very nervous but welcoming hand. Mrs. Nicholson gave her one of her disconcerting head-to-toe examinations, noting the neat school blazer with quite a benign nod.

'I — I wanted to say — ' this startling new Sam stammered out, 'if — if it *was* my fault you fell downstairs I'm very, very sorry . . . '

'You were running about in a silly panic over nothing. But that was all, Samantha. I quite understand it was an accident. All water under the bridge now, my dear! We'll forget all about it, shall we?'

Sam looked as though she couldn't quite believe the 'my dear'. I wasn't sure I could either.

It wasn't an easy evening. Mrs. Nicholson asked difficult questions: was the book coming along, had 'that girl' packed and gone (she wasn't pleased to learn Abigail's absence was just temporary), was Mr. Bassett — the gardener/handyman with the 'busted foot' — still shirking his duties, because she had one too and she certainly didn't intend shirking hers? . . .

But she obviously was very tired, and went to bed early ('Just this once!' she stressed.) Of course, the arrangements in the transformed study came in for some criticism. 'Quite ridiculous! — I could have hopped up the stairs somehow — and if you had to put a bed in here it would have been better along that wall!'

It fell to me to help her settle in the disputed bed. I explained, 'Alex did all this — he's been a real tower of strength here.'

'Well. So he should be.' She dismissed Alex's contribution abruptly. 'Rachel, I haven't asked about your father. Is it all right to leave him back in London?'

'Oh yes. Thank you, he's much better. And my Aunt calls in all the time — and Sam and I keep sending cards and photos.'

'Good. But as soon as I'm properly on my feet, you must pop home for a few days,' she insisted. 'And how has Rick been getting along while I was away?'

'Oh — most of the time very busy with the book,' I said with considerable exaggeration.

'Excellent. And — er — can I ask you, when he took you home that weekend — did he stay over with you?'

'We asked him to stay. He had other arrangements — with a friend.'

She nodded, her lips tightly pursed. I believed she suspected a private assignation somewhere with Abigail. Deep waters which it was best to avoid.

When finally I left her, propped on her pillows with a bell to ring in case of need ('Ridiculous!' she labelled that again) she gave my hand an unexpected squeeze.

'You're a good little soul, Rachel. I'm very pleased to have you here.'

I wondered if she would still be as pleased if she knew my feelings for her adored Rick — that he was my adored Rick too. Needless to say, she didn't ring her bell overnight.

It was the very next day that our visitors were due for lunch. I tried to help Liz, who was fuming about the household growing even larger. For the moment, cold chicken and salad, lemon-meringue dessert ferried in by Alex, wasn't really too difficult. For one horrific moment I thought we were out of Earl Grey.

Just past noon, a sleek grey car drew up in the Gull Cliff courtyard. Peering behind the kitchen curtains, Liz and I appraised the arrivals together: as Alex had hinted, Ralph Kingston was a heavily built man with commanding features and thinning dark hair, who looked as though he was late for this board meeting and in a hurry to reach the next one. He even had a briefcase with him as well as his overnight luggage. Perhaps it was a wonder he hadn't brought a fax machine.

His daughter Georgina seemed to have brought enough baggage for six months. She looked more than her eighteen years, I thought: lankily tall and thin, her dark hair clawed into a knot high on her head. She wore an ankle-length black skirt, a skimpy crocheted black top, and assorted beads and bangles.

'I don't believe it, *another* Lady Muck!' Liz exploded. 'Do you reckon this one will want breakfast in bed?'

Alex had gone out to receive the guests, and I saw what looked like some rather cool handshakes. When Rick appeared to usher them inside, Alex trailed behind weighed down with Georgina's baggage.

I didn't join the family lunch-table. I felt Liz needed both assisting and restraining. We served up the meal without a hitch.

A while later I came upon a carton bulging with books belonging to Georgina, which had been left lying beside the drive. I staggered with it upstairs, and up the steep attic staircase to the upper storey directly under Gull Cliff's sloping roofs, where the rooms were used for storage and spare sleeping accommodation.

'Hallo?' I tapped on Georgina's door. 'I think these are yours?'

'Oh yes. Shakespeare — and Shaw and Chekov. Thank you, Rachel.'

She had turned the small room, in the space of a couple of hours, into something resembling a jumble-sale. It was fortunate Mrs. Nicholson had problems with stairs.

Georgina enquired curiously, 'Have you been here long? Do you like it?'

'Not long. And yes, this is a beautiful place — '

'Oh, of course, the scenery is all right. I meant, living with The Family.

Do you think they're — Strange?'

She had a way of sprinkling her words with implied capital letters. Her voice was lowered to a dramatic whisper.

I said primly, 'It's not really for me to say. I hope this room suits you? — when your father leaves we could swap around. Anyway, you're not all alone up here, you have Alex just next door.'

'Have I really?' Her face expressed sudden dismay. 'Oh well. I can always lock my door.'

As she was marching past me to the stairs, I grabbed her arm quite forcibly.

'What are you saying? What do you mean by that?'

'Oops!' She clapped a hand to her mouth. 'Silly of me! — of course, you're just Staff — so they wouldn't have told you.'

'Told me *what*?'

'Why don't you ask him,' she suggested, 'if you want to know?' She wriggled free, and went on her way downstairs.

That disparaging label 'just staff' put me in mind of Alex agreeing with my designation 'just his brother' on the first day we met. For myself, for various reasons, I felt far, far more than simply 'hired help' at Gull Cliff.

Annoyed and disturbed, I followed Georgina down.

* * *

Mr. Kingston left the following day. For me, it was no loss. I hadn't taken to the gentleman at all.

There seemed not enough hours in the day for all there was to do: revisions of revisions to '*Chapt. 1*', the children, supporting Liz, and of course 'looking after' Mrs. Nicholson — who would have been horrified to think she needed it. When I did have time to think, it was thrilling to consider what was happening to Sam: she was fast gaining in self-confidence, which in turn enabled her to cope with Jade and Jenna's persecution. She had even bought herself an Italian dictionary, and interrupted their whisperings with matter-of-fact questions, 'How do you spell what you called me?' or 'Can you go a bit slower?'

Their malice, of course, was born of rampant jealousy, because Sam so idolised their father and every day he was helping her piano studies: and because she was actually making friends at The Heights — and especially had much impressed Miss Roberts, Head of the Music Department.

In fact, a whisper that Sam might be given a chance in the imminent 'Festival' became a certainty. My glowing sister announced to the assembled dining-room on Friday, 'I'm playing a solo. Miss Roberts said. And she wants to hear Monday what I've chosen, to see if she agrees.'

'That's wonderful!' I exclaimed. 'Bravo to you, Sammy!'

Jenna muttered sulkily, 'That's not fair. You're not properly at the school!'

Sam retorted with spirit. 'Well,

neither are you, not when you're always travelling all over everywhere — and you're in the Concert too!'

The twins were included in the choir, and also had small parts in a playlet about St. Denna's ubiquitous 'Lady', Jenna's a few lines, Jade's a walk-on. Georgina had rather turned up her long classical nose at all that, but she evidently rated a solo performance of any kind merited attention.

'Super, Sammy! You'll knock 'em cold!' she smiled at her across the table.

As if that weren't enough to stoke the twins' fury, Rick voiced his own approval: 'I knew you'd do it, Sam. And now we've the whole weekend to work some more on the Nocturne . . . '

It dawned on me (and probably on them) that he had known about and helped her with her 'audition'. Sam had conspired with him, and breathed not a word to me. If this brought my own stab of jealousy it quickly passed. Had I not hoped to see Sam's crippling shyness fading, her reliance on me lessening?

Later, I told Mrs. Nicholson about it, and she agreed, 'Just what Samantha needs!' in genuine interest. Unfortunately she wasn't so well today, doubtless because yesterday she had been stumping about the house, even the garden, on tours of inspection. Her own physician, an elderly bespectacled gentleman, had been in to see her. He directed Alex and me, 'You *must* ensure she rests, please understand that's essential!'

We looked at one another glumly. We understood Dr. Grant's orders. He wasn't explaining to us how to carry them out.

Tonight, Mrs. Nicholson was early in bed, having swallowed her tablets with much tut-tutting. She told me again, she was very pleased about Sam. Also she inferred, with Rick tutoring her, it was bound to happen — but it mustn't distract him from his work.

I felt like asking, 'What work?' because I was struggling on with the book very much on my own. That same evening I tried to give the task another hour, now inconveniently parked in the conservatory until the study was free again. There were too many distractions here, people to-ing and fro-ing, the drifting sounds of the television, Sam's piano practice. The twins should be in bed, but they weren't. Well, I had only one pair of hands! Georgina Kingston hadn't yet lifted a beringed finger. As for Liz quite simply she was nearing breaking point . . .

'Coffee break!' Alex said, and set a cup down beside me.

I looked gratefully up at him, but the smile he returned wasn't his old smile. It was just as kind, as gentle, but there was a bleakness in it. I knew he had telephoned London a couple of times today about the accountancy partnership he hoped to join in the autumn — it seemed to have run into problems. But for his Grandmother's illness, I believed he would be well on his way from Cornwall — and from me — by now, to try to rescue the plan.

I hated to think I had caused him pain. I missed the closeness we had shared.

There was really little more I could do to the manuscript until I sorted out various points with Rick. He and Sam were still busy in the music-room: I put my head round the door to tell her it was past bedtime, and she nodded obediently and wished Rick a shy, happy 'Good night!'

I added, 'Rick, I need to see you, please. I'm stuck fast with the book.'

'Tomorrow,' he said wearily.

'Well, all right. But it isn't working out, the dates are all mixed up — '

'Tomorrow we'll look at it. Please?'

'All right,' I agreed again grudgingly. I had been fobbed off like that before.

He was frowning as he turned away to close the piano. As his farewell smile for Sam faded, his face seemed deeply shadowed. It happened often — and every time I could only long vainly to soothe the pain I couldn't understand.

Tonight, I couldn't let it happen again. I held his arm as he was turning to the door.

'Rick — I wanted to thank you very much for helping Sam . . . '

His eyes looked into mine. The room was very still: through the arched window was a balmy summer night, with an early star or two pinpointing their distant light. He didn't shake off that detaining hand.

'I wish I could do something to help you too.' I whispered. 'I — I just can't bear to see you so unhappy . . . '

My voice was starting to shake. I was aware then of his arm around me, drawing me close to him.

'Rachel, you're very kind. Very sweet . . . and I'm so sorry I make you unhappy too . . . '

In an unreal sunburst of joy I clung to him, with all my strength, with all my love. Gently his hand lifted my face, and then his lips were touching my hair, my brow, and my own waiting lips. Warm and strong was the lingering kiss he gave me. Its warmth and its strength almost were pain.

'Rachel,' he said softly. The way he spoke my name, the way no-one else ever had spoken it. And then again, 'Rachel . . . please forgive . . . '

What was he asking me to forgive him? For causing me sadness and concern? Or for that caress that had left me drained, a being bewitched and entranced?

I was alone in the room, the door closing quietly behind him. It was a long time before I could bring myself to move, to break the dream-like spell.

Upstairs, I found all was very quiet now. Long after Sam had fallen into blissful slumber, I lay for many hours wide awake — living over and over the touch of Rick's lips on mine. When it was almost dawn I slept heavily — and woke with a start to greet the morning somehow.

Yesterday was utterly unreal. Yet, carrying an early tea-tray to Mrs.

Nicholson, I felt the imprint of those wondrous moments must be written clear upon my flushed face.

As it happened, she scarcely glanced at me. Sitting bolt upright, she had most of the contents of her familiar capacious handbag spread out on her bed.

'Good morning,' I started to say. 'It looks like another sunny — '

Really, there was nothing sunny about this morning.

'Rachel, come here, please! I know I'm getting to be a cantankerous old woman. I hope I'm not completely losing my grip . . . Can you see a purse here?'

I whispered, 'No. No purse.'

'This jeweller's box, I keep a very old diamond filigree brooch in it — it was my mother's.'

'The — the box is empty. I can see.'

'Yes, it's empty. Which means someone came in here last night. Those tablets I took would make you sleep through the Last Trump! — '

Far, far away now was my wondrous dream. In pure horror I blurted out, 'Mrs. Nicholson, I know I was the last one to say goodnight to you, but I hope you don't think I— '

'No, no. I don't. I want you to help me, Rachel, before I make this public.' Her voice was sharp, but its sharpness wasn't for me: I met directly the unfaded piercing blue gaze of eyes very angry, very troubled. 'Please have a look round the house — doors, windows. I'm sure you'll find nothing, we've an efficient alarm system here as you know. Any intruder would need to be a technical genius!'

'I'll look right away! But — if it's not a burglary, that means . . . '

'I know what it means. We'll consider that when we need to,' she said grimly.

Ten minutes later I was back at her bedside. My report was just as she expected. Nothing had been disturbed, no-one else was complaining of an overnight theft.

'Was there very much in the purse, Mrs. Nicholson?'

'Yes, as it happens. I sent Rick to the bank for me while I was in the Hospital — in case I was immobilised for some time . . . but the money isn't important. The brooch is irreplaceable.'

I would have felt the same. That she shared the feeling showed she was not so wholly unsentimental as she liked people to think.

I couldn't imagine how she meant to handle this situation. Wholly in character, she met it head-on. She appeared at the Saturday morning breakfast table, her white hair neatly coiled, her head erect. At the end of the meal, she summoned Liz in to join us. To the audience of five adults and three children, she made her announcement.

'During the night, some items were removed from my handbag. Money and jewellery. I needn't say how upset and grieved I am that *someone* in this house . . . '

There were gasps and mutterings. Liz's eyes were rounded like saucers. Georgina almost seemed thrilled by this dramatic variation on the Gull Cliff routine. Rick was deeply frowning — and so I saw was Alex, rare deep lines creasing his forehead.

'Today I intend to sit quietly in my room.' Mrs. Nicholson went on, her eyes moving from face to face. 'If the person concerned comes to return the items to me, I shall take the matter no further. Otherwise — I shan't let the matter rest. I give you all fair warning!'

No-one spoke. No-one moved. The old lady prompted sharply, 'Will somebody kindly pass me some toast?'

* * *

Throughout the day suspense was poised over the household like some hovering bird of prey waiting to sink accusing talons into one or other of us.

People reacted in their different ways. The twins giggled together in corners, seeming to feel that Great-Gran had lots of money and jewellery anyway — but it was mean of someone when she was ill. In contrast, Sam stood around in obvious terror of being questioned — and so looked downright guilty, except no-one in their right minds would suspect her. But it was later in the day, when I overheard Georgina making a dramatic phone call, that my anxiety reached new bounds.

'Mummy? — it's Georgie! . . . Mummy, the most *horrendous* thing . . . at Dead of Night, while we were all sleeping — Great-Auntie's handbag . . . yes, not just money, this *priceless* Family Heirloom . . . ' I missed some words, though by now I was shamelessly listening. I heard all too well her final outpouring. 'Yes, of course, Mummy, but no-one's said anything yet — only *everyone* must have guessed . . . Well, when we all

KNOW we've got some Sticky Fingers in the family, wouldn't you think she'd lock up her things? . . . '

She lowered her voice then. I wasn't sure I wanted to know more.

And yet not knowing was its own kind of torture — so that when I spotted her alone soon after, I had to plunge straight in.

'Excuse me! I overheard you talking. WHO in this house has sticky fingers?'

She looked startled, but not averse to passing on interesting family scandal.

'Hasn't anyone told you, Rachel? Oh, but they wouldn't, because you're just — '

'I know, I'm not Family, I'm Staff — you told me before! That was when you dropped nasty hints about locking your room as you're next-door to Alex! And just now you were telling your mother Mrs. Nicholson must know she ought to lock up her things! — '

'Did I say that? Well, it's true.' She leant her head confidentially nearer mine. 'I've heard my parents discussing it all. Dad thinks it's disgraceful — quite juicy stuff! To start with, you know Alex was Uncle Rick's Manager for quite a time? — '

'I know that. Until they had some sort of quarrel.'

'Not just a quarrel, far worse than that! All the money side of things was left to him. And he was just *helping himself*, robbing Uncle Rick right and left!'

Had I really known or guessed what was coming? I couldn't have done, because I knew Alex. I said flatly, 'I don't believe a word of it.'

'It's true! Gospel truth! Dad called it 'creative accounting'!'

Yes, the Ralph Kingston I had briefly met would call it that. I repeated, 'I still don't believe it.'

She leant closer, almost with a certain glee. 'Well, doctoring the books wasn't *all* he did. Rachel, did you ever see a picture of Auntie Tina? — Uncle Rick's wife? — '

As I gazed at her, it seemed my

blood already chilled had turned to ice.

'They keep the pictures hidden mostly, but take my word for it,' Georgie rattled on, 'she was really lovely! And — all the while poor Uncle Rick was busy playing his piano and losing his money — they were Having an Affair. How about that?'

The appalling words came out with some relish. Before I could even summon voice to answer, the sudden full opening of a half-open window beside us made both of us leap a foot in the air.

'Georgina!' Mrs. Nicholson's eyes were blue steel. 'I'll speak to you inside, if you please! — Rachel, have you some work to be doing?'

The window shut again abruptly. It was foolish of us, of course, to tittle-tattle directly outside the study now transformed to a bedroom.

An apprehensive Georgina went off indoors. I didn't envy her. But at this stunned moment, my mind had fastened on one very glaring omission.

Mrs. Nicholson had NOT rebuked Georgie, 'Don't talk such rubbish!' She had NOT ordered me, 'Pay no attention, they're all groundless rumours!' Why had she uttered no such denial?

I lingered a few minutes in the garden before I could face going in. Gull Cliff looked at its most idyllic, its blue shutters matching the sky, all around the colours of flowers, the sound of the tide, the plaints of wheeling sea-birds. A place of great beauty — but back across the years these walls must have known more sorrow and bitterness than I never dreamed.

With great pain I thought now of Alex, the man I had trusted in this house of strangers, who had from my first uncertain days here given me strength and comfort. I couldn't and wouldn't believe the sordid accusations against him! — and yet, having heard them, knowing his own close family believed them, could I ever completely trust him again? . . .

And for Rick, who last night so unbelievably had held me in his arms, I knew now why no photographs of Christina graced the walls of Gull Cliff. If indeed he had lost her twice, or believed he had — once in death, once in supposed betrayal of his love — how could he bear to look upon her face? And the children she had borne him must be a daily reminder of her, a daily deepening of pain.

For such a man as Riccardo Corelli there would be no forgiving or forgetting, no kindly softening of time.

Eventually I went back into the house. And indeed, it was easy to bury myself in work, because I found Liz flopped on a chair in the kitchen, pronouncing herself too shattered by the idea of a thief creeping into Mrs. Nicholson's bedroom to face up to the day's chores. As the hours dragged by, no-one confessed to rifling that handbag. Hardly surprising, but it meant suspicions were still rife: and apart from the mutterings about Alex, it seemed the fingers were pointing straight at Liz herself.

That wasn't surprising either. I knew she disliked Mrs. Nicholson, and complained about being paid 'a pittance' to cope with an ever increasing workload. As well, lately she had grumbled constantly about lack of free time to see Stevie in the village.

Yet I couldn't really believe this of Liz, that even in a major fit of pique she would try to 'get back at' the old lady like this — and help on her own financial woes in so shameful a fashion. I had come to know her quite well, as we were both 'Staff' — as Miss Georgina would hasten to remind us. Liz wasn't over-bright, but she was well-meaning and *transparent*. Had she really committed this miserable act. I felt I would have known.

This most traumatic of days still had another shot left in its locker. In the evening Abigail rang from London and

Rick took the call in the lounge: from my new work-place in the adjoining conservatory I heard bits and pieces. It seemed Miss Horton had a couple of autumn concerts 'in the bag', she wanted Rick to begin work for them right away — 'but *not* in that mad-house, Ricco!' Her voice raised in annoyance came to me quite clearly through the half-open door.

It probably sounded a mad-house. The twins were squabbling noisily, Liz seemed to be having shrill words with Georgie, Sam was blissfully practising scales. On this sultry night, doors stood open everywhere.

I heard Rick briefly telling the tale of the missing valuables, and her response that sounded like, 'This'll be that shifty brother of yours again? — WHY do you have the guy under your roof?' Which could only mean Rick had already told her the family history? I thought angrily, what business was it of hers? . . .

The rest of their conversation was all too easily pieced together. She was pressing him to leave the Gull Cliff 'pandemonium' and stay at her London flat as long as need by while he prepared for the concerts unhindered. The chance to return to the concert platform must in no way be jeopardised.

She would get the flat sorted out. She would come down to fetch him. Sooner rather than later.

As though the idea of Rick going away at all wasn't shattering enough, this picture of a cosy twosome at Abigail's flat was beyond bearing. As well, I was *angry* enough at Miss Horton's arrogant arrangement of other people's lives to march straight through to the lounge, where Rick was sharing the sofa with an unopened newspaper and Georgie studying a play.

'Excuse me!' I confronted him. 'Are you going off to London to live? Soon?'

He glanced at me with a lift of expressive brows. Evidently he didn't consider it worthwhile discussing a small matter of eavesdropping.

'Possibly I may go. Why are you

asking?' The words were distant: last night was a million miles away.

'Why? Well, did you forget we're working on the book?' I didn't bother with finesse. 'I suppose your new Manager doesn't think that's important! — '

'Not very.'

'Well, I do! Rick, you do too, if you think about it! We've both slaved over that book — it's not exactly taking shape, but it looks like it might! . . . And you *did* engage me for the whole summer, remember? And my sister's settled down at school here! *And* I've given the use of my house to relatives till September! . . . '

The protests poured out in near desperation. So clearly I could see my work and my stay here fading like a puff of smoke . . . everything ending, my love, my life, everything! Perhaps it was the panic in my voice that attracted an audience. For whatever reason, we had one. Any moment Mrs. Nicholson would add to its number on her crutches.

'Rachel, we'll discuss this later!' Rick said with rising anger to match my own. 'Anyway, don't upset yourself. I'm sure you'll be adequately compensated.'

I was near to shouting at him that I wanted neither his patronising nor his compensating. But at this same instant there came without warning a lurid shimmer of lightning through the room, and an almost instantaneous thunder-clap, rending the night sky with its violence, seeming to lift the roof of the big house from its quaking walls.

It made all of us almost leap out of our skins. The twins let out a scream and clung to each other, Liz rushed in from the kitchen. But it was the effect on Rick that was most strange and disturbing: his face had turned an unnatural grey-white, he staggered like a drunken man and put up both hands to his forehead.

I started forward, but other supporting hands reached him first. Gently, firmly, Alex caught hold of him. It was the first, the only time I had seen the two of them close together: it emphasised Alex's taller stature, the clear pale blue of his eyes that were filled now with concern.

'It's all right, Rick. You're all right. Will you go upstairs and lie down?'

I expected that sustaining hold to be flung off. That didn't happen. Rick looked totally dazed, unaware even of where he was or who was helping him.

As his brother led him gently away, he was passive and unresisting. Alex glanced at me to whisper, 'Please could you get the kids to bed, Rachel?'

I whispered back. 'Of course. Can you manage? — is there anything I can — ?'

'Don't worry. It'll pass.'

This was the first time I had spoken to Alex directly since Georgie confided to me those unpleasant family scandals. I scarcely knew how to look at him. But we were both too concerned about Rick to take notice.

The other thought hammering at my

mind was the memory of Aunt Doreen's solemn warnings back in London. She had watched Rick carefully. She had training and experience, she was sure there was some sort of serious problem. I had chosen then not to listen to her.

Somehow the twins were extinguished in their beds. After that one mighty thunder-clap the storm rumbled on sulkily for a while then faded into the distance. The household showed signs of settling down. When I peeped in on Mrs. Nicholson she was actually fast asleep — which showed how greatly the strains of today had affected her.

Sam, stealing borrowed time, was still blissfully busy with the piano. When I went in to banish her to bed, she showed me what she was working on: it was all, 'Miss Roberts thinks this' and 'Rick taught me that', in hushed excitement. I was thrilled for her. I wondered too what it would do to her if, almost without warning, Rick moved off to London — and Sam and

I, both riding so high on our respective pink clouds, bumped down to earth.

We both looked round quite guiltily when the door opened. The lamp on the piano made a magical circle of light in the dim room.

'Oh! — Rick. I'm sorry — were we disturbing you?' I said confusedly. 'Sammy, shut up shop, off to bed!'

She glanced up with a smiling 'Good night!' as she passed him. As I was awkwardly following her out, he said unexpectedly, '*You* don't have to go — do you?'

'Oh.' I said again. Our mutual flashpoint of anger seemed an age ago. 'No, I don't. Are you feeling better? — was it the sudden noise, or — ?'

'I'm well. Grazie. Thank you.'

It wasn't convincing. His face still looked haggard, his black hair was tumbled over his forehead. He sat down on the piano-stool Sam had just vacated, and I watched in awed fascination as one hand reached out to touch the keys as though in infinite longing. It drew back without making a sound. The straying fingers were shaking.

Yesterday, he had held me so gloriously in his arms and kissed me. And now, in the quiet of this haunted room, in the warm summer darkness and the solitude of our two selves, my arms were around him, drawing him near to me. I whispered, 'Rick . . . if it would help to talk — to tell me . . . oh, you can tell me anything in the world, because . . . '

I didn't quite say, 'Because I love you.' He must know that.

He didn't answer the jumbled words. But he responded to my arms, he clung to me. I cradled his dark head, smoothing back his hair, and then my face was against his. The warmth and nearness of him filled all my being.

I breathed softly again, 'Try to tell me . . . why you're so frightened to play, is it because playing makes you forget? — or remember? . . . '

Startled, he drew back a little. But still he was holding fast to me. He said quite clearly, 'I remember. I almost remember. And — dear God, I *mustn't* remember . . . '

The words were like a sob of despair. I ached for his unknown pain, and caressed him, and loved him.

It ended quite slowly and gently. He seemed to understand suddenly who we were, where we were, whose arms were holding him. With tenderness he loosed my hands, and then like yesterday his lips sought mine, warmly, fondly. I couldn't catch the words he said.

The door opened and closed. I went on standing there in the silent room. My arms were empty, but still they felt the living nearness of him.

Somehow I would find a way to reach him, to help him. In my love for him I would.

And my heart soared in the knowledge that he cared for me even a little. He did care for me.

5

'How are you today, Mrs. Nicholson?' I asked.

The question scarcely needed answering. As I helped her haul herself up in bed, the face I had thought would once have been beautiful — as Rick's mother's probably was beautiful — looked tired and aged.

But her voice still was strong and direct: 'I'm as well as I can be, thank you — in the circumstances.'

'I know. I'm so sorry. We haven't found out about the money and the — '

'We haven't!' she agreed grimly. 'Though I have my ideas, and I'm not often mistaken. Rachel, don't run away. I want to speak to you.'

I turned back, aware my face was glowing, suddenly wondering if she somehow had knowledge of those moments I shared with Rick. But this was another matter. It was one almost as difficult to confront.

'Yesterday Georgie was talking to you about Alex. She's a silly girl, she gets real life mixed up with her dramas! She has no business to go around spreading gossip and digging up dirt!'

'I didn't believe what she said. Not one word of it.'

'Well, I'm glad to hear it,' she approved, and coughed. 'Rachel, the whole family were very upset around the time poor Tina died. A lot of things were thought and said. The — the *truth* has never really been discovered — so don't let that silly girl tell you it has! And I hope you'll treat the whole matter in strict confidence?'

'Of course,' I agreed readily. 'Of course I will.'

Still she hadn't given me the flat denial about Alex I so expected and wanted. In effect, hadn't she told me simply to keep my mind wide open and my mouth tight shut?

It was some half-hour later that she appeared at the Sunday breakfast table. She ordered, 'Liz, I want a few words with you, please!' I sensed poor Liz would get away less lightly this morning than I had.

'I believe you went into Penmoryn yesterday, on the bus? And you came back here with some new clothes and shoes — from Mallory's, isn't that right?'

Liz muttered, 'How do you know I did? You were sitting in your room all day!'

'I have my sources. Are you denying you went shopping there?'

Meeting Liz's eyes, I shook my head: I had seen her come in with interesting carrier-bags from that far from inexpensive store — but definitely I *wasn't* one of the informing 'sources'. Indeed, I hadn't even linked the shopping spree with the missing money.

It seemed other people had. For a moment Liz stood still, as the implied accusation dawned on her. When it did, her reactions were drastic. She dumped the tray she was holding forcibly down on the table, scattering crockery in confusion.

'If you're saying I took your money — well, I never did!' She rounded fiercely on Mrs. Nicholson. 'I saved up for those things! — except the dress, Stevie bought me that ready for my birthday . . . and — and I've had enough of working here, you never liked me, you always moaned at me, and — now you can find someone else to moan at! I'm leaving *now*!'

Tears started as she fled from the room, crashing the door behind her. I wondered which of the shocked group around the table had 'grassed' about the carrier-bags. Possibly the twins, it would be right up their street. Possibly Georgina, who was trying to mop a flood of fruit juice from her lap.

'Well, good riddance!' she gave her opinion. 'But shouldn't she be made to return the things to the shop? Why don't we ring them and sort it all out? — '

'I don't think so, Georgina,' Mrs. Nicholson said icily. 'This family has washed enough dirty linen in public. Let the girl go. I'll find a replacement. Will you please clean up this mess, Rachel?'

As I started on that, I noticed Alex slip away upstairs in the wake of Liz. Before the interrupted meal was finished, both of them reappeared. He was carrying her largest suitcase — she must have tumbled her things into it in heaps — and coaxing her, 'Let me drive you! — come on, Liz, I'll just get the car out — '

'I don't want any favours! I can ring my boyfriend to pick me up. And whoever you get in place of me, good luck to her!'

'Just one moment, miss,' Mrs. Nicholson called out to her. 'You're in a great hurry to leave us. I'm still missing my property — so I think someone had better look through your things before you run away. Georgie, will you — ?'

Georgina jumped up with alacrity. I was squirming now with the sheer unpleasantness of the scene. Liz was starting to cry again — and once more it was Alex who put a protective arm round her and turned to confront his Grandmother.

'Gran, hold on. I don't think you've any right. Liz gave me her word she isn't taking anything away that isn't hers — I've helped her pack, there weren't any bundles of banknotes! — '

'Well, that's nonsense! — they could be in her bag, or stuffed in her clothes,' Georgie challenged. 'Anyway, we all know how much *your* word is worth, Alessandro Corelli! . . . '

That made me jump, my first knowledge of his wholly unexpected full name. Alex just looked at her with narrowed eyes.

Under cover of that exchange, Liz had escaped to the door. It was pleasing to me that Sam spoke up timidly, 'Bye,

Liz! — Sorry you're going!' No-one echoed the sentiment. Across the table, Rick scarcely seemed interested. Mrs. Nicholson said shortly that she would be contacting Liz's mother.

I went outside to find Alex loading the luggage into his car. Liz was already huddled on the back seat, scrubbing at her eyes with a tissue.

I asked her anxiously, 'Will you be all right? Have you somewhere to go?'

Alex answered for her, 'I'm taking her to Stevie's place, I'll have a word with his Dad. And she says there could be a part-time job in their art shop, the one on the corner called 'The Picture Gallery' . . . '

'That would be nice, Liz,' I encouraged. 'Better than skivvying here! Look, if you need any help, promise you'll ring us! — or get Stevie to ring us? — '

Again Alex answered, 'I've already told her. We're here if ever she wants us.'

The '*us*' meant Alex and me. That was strange. Strange that we both had used that small telling word.

As the car drove off, I reflected too that this left Gull Cliff minus one dubious but most essential domestic worker. I had a nasty presentiment about who would be filling the gap.

I was already up to my eyes in the kitchen when Alex returned from St. Denna. He told me he had chatted to Stevie's widowed father and elder sister, and they seemed nice friendly people. Liz could have their spare room as long as was needed.

I glanced up from the hasty concoction of an apple dessert.

'Good. She wasn't a domestic marvel but she's had a rough time here. I do feel your Gran has been very hard on poor Liz . . . and you were very kind to her. Alex.'

'Oh.' He waved a dismissive hand. 'So were you.'

'No, today I just sat there and let it happen. It was you who said they had no right to search her . . . ' I stopped there in confusion. Other people might well assume he had personal reasons for intervening — like the searching process being extended all round the household.

He smiled at me as though fully understanding what I was thinking. I said abruptly, 'I know Liz quite well, I just don't see her as a very mean and sneaky thief!'

'Nor do I. Which poses the question — if she *isn't*, someone else is?'

'Maybe no-one is! I was thinking, Mrs. Nicholson isn't at all herself at present, since her accident. Couldn't she just possibly have put the things away somewhere and forgotten about it?'

'That's an idea. You're right, it's not like her to behave the way she did — so, who knows?' He raised his eyes ceilingwards. 'Here, let me peel those apples.'

As I passed them over, there was one other thing I had to say to him. It was even harder than discussing theft and dishonour with a man labelled by his own kin as guilty of both.

'Last night, when there was the storm — I saw how Rick nearly collapsed.'

'I know. He has a horror of thunder.'

'It was much worse than that, wasn't it? Alex, I think — he could be a very sick man?'

He said soberly, 'Between the two of us, I've written off to Dr. Bergmann — he's supposed to understand the problem. I've asked him to come down here.'

'Have you really?' I breathed in real awe. 'Won't Rick be *furious* with you?'

He shrugged his shoulders. 'Nothing new in that. — Okay, Chef, what's next after the apples?'

As a combined operation, we produced Sunday lunch. And as I had foreseen, that was to set a pattern for the following days. For me they were all such a rush — with all the extra chores, the invalid Mrs. Nicholson who wasn't so well (plus a fifth, maybe sixth, rewrite of that never-ending *Chapt. 1*) — that it seemed I could neither breathe nor think. Quite simply, I had to take each day as it came. Often I worked alongside Alex, we chatted a little — but I was painfully aware of a barrier between us, so many things left unsaid on either side.

Just briefly. I worked with Rick. He was quiet, gentle, but very distant and pre-occupied. He was impossible to reach.

It was on Wednesday that the children returned late from school after 'rehearsals', full of their own dramatic news. Miss Roberts, the Head of Music of whom I had heard so much — and an essential accompanist for the very imminent School Show — had suddenly been laid low with suspected appendicitis. It was lucky that her deputy, Mrs. Cross, could take her place.

'But the timing for the ballet dancing went all wrong. Mariella Bourne told me,' Sam confided, proud of her new friendship with the budding young ballerina.

The twins chimed in, '*And* the choir singing, it was horrible! And she missed out a whole chunk!'

'Well, give her a chance. It must be awful to get thrown in at the last minute,' I sympathised. 'At least she has all day tomorrow to get it right!'

Only one full day, in fact. The school's 'Musical Entertainment' was actually this coming Friday. I was developing more stage fright on Sam's behalf than she was for herself. Her quite serene attitude was. 'Rick thinks I'll be all right — so I shall.' The twins' dark mutterings didn't seem to upset her.

Thursday brought excitement still greater. I answered the phone soon after eleven to be greeted by Sam's voice, shaky with tension.

'Ray, it's me! . . . I'm ringing from Miss Jesmond's room, she let me! . . . Ray, something *frightful* happened this morning. Mrs. Cross was doing something to the stage, and — and she fell off the steps, and — '

'Don't tell me!'

'Yes, we think she might have broken something, anyway she's still at the hospital . . . and *someone*'s got to play all the piano music tomorrow, so I said I knew someone who could do it with their eyes shut . . . '

I exclaimed in panic, 'I'd love to help, but — I'm so out of practice, I'm not sure — '

'No, I didn't mean you. Though I bet you could do it,' she asserted loyally.

Now I was even more aghast. 'Sam! You haven't really told them — '

Obviously, she really had. She was ringing now to find out if Rick was home, and if so I must keep him home. The hard-pressed Principal of The Heights would drive over right away to approach him in person.

Rick *was* home, I said. But Sam had no right at all to volunteer him. I couldn't imagine what trouble it could cause! She answered quite cheerily, 'He'll do it! If we ask him right. If

I ask him he will, you'll see.'

Perhaps I had been better off with my shy young sister of a few months ago who seldom opened her mouth. This time she had opened it once too often! Of course, she had no idea of all those sinister mysteries surrounding the abrupt end to Riccardo Corelli's musical career.

In this sudden new crisis I wondered, should I consult Alex? — should I tell Rick myself so at least he had fair warning? I ended up doing neither — for as though there weren't problems enough, at this moment a car arrived on the courtyard driven by a tall figure with a glorious suntan and an upswept knot of golden-blonde hair. Abigail Horton appeared to have been poured into her immaculately white jeans. There was no denying she topped the glamour stakes around Gull Cliff.

'Hi!' she called to me. 'How are you, Rachel?'

I mumbled, 'Fine, thanks, are you? . . . I'm not sure if your room is ready — we lost Liz, you see — '

'I know. I missed all the fun, didn't I? — and still no-one's handed back the loot!' (Which comment meant Rick must have kept in close touch with her while she was away? . . .) 'Is Ricco around? I've some news for him!'

I said stonily, 'He's in the garden.'

'Right! Oh, and a drink would be nice. Something in a tall glass with plenty of ice.'

I felt like answering 'Yes ma'am!' and saluting smartly. I watched her walk round the side of the house, hardly aware how deeply I was frowning. She was here as the Manager of a renowned musician — but even more as a beautiful assured woman with ideas about her client far from merely professional.

'Is that car whose I think it is?' a quiet voice was asking beside me.

'Abigail. She's back! Giving out her orders like there's no tomorrow.' I looked round at Alex — and again the urge came to seek his help. Only the stage of discussion was past.

'And whose car is this black one? — we're popular today!' he was commenting mildly.

I breathed, 'Good grief, she's not here already! . . . ' I saw Miss Jesmond's vehicle gliding to a halt beside Abigail's, with a bright and eager Sam sitting next to the Principal: like the last time I saw her, it struck me that she was surprisingly informal and unassuming — but today her pleasant face was distinctly harrassed.

'Good morning.' She spoke to Alex, who had moved politely forward to receive her. 'Miss Jesmond — from the school! I need to see Mr. Corelli rather urgently — '

'Oh dear, is something wrong with Sam? — ' Alex started to ask, but the half-posed question wasn't answered. She was eyeing him doubtfully.

'Er — you're not — ?'

'No. Just his brother,' he explained, as always.

'Yes, of course. It's Mr. Riccardo

Corelli I need to see . . . '

I thought he muttered to me, 'The story of my life.' Aloud, he suggested pleasantly, 'I think he's in the garden, shall I take you round, Miss Jesmond?'

An excited Sam pranced behind them. Wholly uninvited I followed on too — only I was far from prancing.

* * *

'Well, of course, I appreciate it's a lot to ask,' Miss Jesmond said. Perched on one of the white scrollwork chairs, she looked quite young, distinctly nervous. 'But I'm really desperate! Some of our guests are coming quite a distance . . . well, you do see I'm in big trouble! Of course, we can present a show of sorts. But Miss Roberts' role was essential, the accompaniments for the singing and dancing and the recorder group, and — and . . . '

She trailed into silence, and no-one helped her. Rick was looking at her in open disbelief. I saw Abigail had some papers spread on the table, noticeably an airline timetable.

'Well,' Miss Jesmond began again with what seemed here favourite introduction. 'Mrs. Cross should be back from Casualty soon, so she could explain the whole programme. She could go through it all with you, Mr. Corelli! So — if you came along *now* you could rehearse this afternoon with the ballet girls and the choir . . . ?'

Rick said nothing at all. He still looked like a man having a bad dream — or who just wanted to run away. Suddenly I wanted to blurt out, 'Don't make him do it! — don't even try to make him! — '

It was Abigail who found authoritative voice to dismiss the whole idea. For one rare moment I was grateful for her presence.

'I'm sorry, Miss Jesmond. I'm Mr. Corelli's Manager . . . I'm afraid this really is quite out of the question. Do you realise *who* you're asking to be your stand-in accompanist?'

The deflated Principal muttered, 'Oh. Oh dear. Yes, of course . . . '

'I can show you a list of his commitments.' Abigail flourished a hand at the papers on the table. 'We're just working out an autumn tour. Over in the States.'

'Of course, I do quite understand.' Miss Jesmond was already easing herself from her chair. 'Forgive me imposing on your time, but you see, I have to clutch at every straw! The event is so very important to all my girls — and to all their families . . . '

I was just opening my mouth to suggest that if a half-trained rusty pianist could help, here I was. The offer never surfaced. Sam, who had been watching on the sidelines, made her shy earnest presence felt.

'Rick.' She tweaked his arm. 'It's only a couple of days. Only a few hours. I *promised* you'd do it for them. I would, if I could . . . '

He looked round rather helplessly at her face alight with all its eager trust.

It would have taken a heart of stone not be moved by her pleading.

'Please? I did promise them. Everyone's worked so hard. *Please*?' she whispered. 'For me? . . . si?'

'If you promised you don't give me much choice, do you? All right. For you — si!'

It took Miss Jesmond a moment to comprehend. Then her face lighted to match Sam's.

'Mr. Corelli, I don't know what to say! Samantha's quite right, it is just a few hours — I do hope it won't really interfere with all your arrangements — '

He shrugged his shoulders, as though disclaiming responsibility for those 'arrangements', for whatever might happen at the school, for Sam's persuasions, for Abigail's angry frown.

'Well, now,' Miss Jesmond swept on, striking while the iron was hot, 'could you manage to come along to the school right away? I'm so hoping Sally Cross will be there soon, poor soul — let's hope she's not too woozy with all her painkillers! . . . '

Before Rick rose from his chair, I actually saw Sam steal an arm round his neck to plant a swift little kiss of gratitude on his cheek and whisper, 'Grazie!' After that, as she glanced round at me, I had the outrageous idea that she winked . . . or could it have been a trick of the light on her staid and innocent glasses?

A still overwhelmed Miss Jesmond drove off — having begged me to convey her apologies to Mrs. Nicholson for rushing away so rudely, but there was so very much to do. Rick's car followed meekly behind. I guessed she was intent on whisking him off before he woke up to what he was doing — or before she woke up herself.

I liked Miss Jesmond. I was very pleased for her. I was pleased too that Abigail had been disconcerted — only this time, so strangely, I was on Abigail's side. Most of all, I was desperately concerned for the man whose despair I watched and tried to understand last night. What today and tomorrow would do, what genies would be let out of their bottles, who could say?

Even more now I wanted to consult Alex, but there was no chance: he was doing something to the lily-pool at his Grandmother's behest, and she had come out to supervise from a nearby seat. At least it seemed Alex had broken the news about the school — something I had been wholeheartedly dreading: I heard him say, 'He'll be okay, Gran!' and 'Might even do him good!' — and 'How did all these frogs get themselves into this pond? . . . '

Presently I collected the girls from The Heights, and was much tempted to march straight in to reconnoitre, but in cowardly fashion waited at the gates. The twins emerged looking very sulky: they reported that Rick was in the Big Hall with a limp and bandaged Mrs. Cross and Mariella Bourne, rehearsing her special ballet scene which was one of the show's highlights.

'It's not fair. He's our Daddy. Sam had to go and push in, didn't she? We'd have told Old Mother Jesmond! . . . '

Sam, quite oblivious, looked to be living in a blissful dream. I wished I could have shared it, that a glimpse of Rick's car parked in a corner didn't fill me with apprehension.

It was quite late in the evening when that car returned to Gull Cliff. He came into the house slowly, his face very weary. The evening meal was cleared away, but I had kept his share back: I said awkwardly, 'You're late, you must be starving! Just sit down and — '

'I'm not hungry. I think I had something at the school.'

'You look quite exhausted!' Mrs. Nicholson said severely. 'Rick, I can easily telephone Kate Jesmond and explain you're not able to help her after all.'

At this belated stage I piped up, 'I'd do it instead! — I could probably scrape through it!'

Rick said shortly, 'Is this a conspiracy? I'd just like to be left alone — do you mind?'

He went straight up to his room. He had some notes to study. I didn't quite dare to disturb him.

It was a very close and clammy night, and a disturbed one. Jade had a stomachache and Jenna an earache — or so they insisted, maybe to gain some attention. Sam kept on waking up and asking, 'Is it morning? — you won't let me sleep late?' Mrs. Nicholson actually rang her bell for the first time ever because she had spilt some water on her pillow. She was furious with herself for ringing — and with me for answering and making her feel beholden.

The morning did come, with a heavy sky, an eerie stillness even here on our breezy perch above the sea. The kitchen radio crackled ominously.

No work was being done at the school today. When I drove the girls in, festoons of bunting and multi-coloured balloons were on show, a red and white striped marquee would presently be dispensing refreshments. Displays of work had been set up in the classrooms.

Sam rushed inside, with a brief ' 'Bye!' before I could wish her good luck.

Back at the house the aura of excitement was, if anything, even more evident. An array of sandwiches and salad was laid out in the dining-room which no-one wanted. Everyone was making phone calls — Georgie chattering to 'Mummy', Rick talking volubly across the miles, as he sometimes did, to his Uncle Cesare in their soft musical tongue — and Abigail ringing, it seemed all and sundry. As she hadn't succeeded in preventing to-day, she was organising everything.

'I'll drive you, Ricky. Have you eaten something? — are you sure? Don't stand for any hassles with last minute changes! . . . Come on, we've time for a quiet coffee in the garden, just you and little me, caro mio! . . . '

I made their 'quiet coffee'. I watched the completely possessive way she led him off, smiling straight into his face. Today she was wearing a slender floaty dress in a pure azure that exactly matched her eyes. The sun glinted on her blonde hair scattering half-bared shoulders. She might have stepped out of a glossy fashion mag — with no intention of stepping back in.

'I'll phone Leland Ellison back about the New York date,' she was going on, as they rounded the house. 'Oh, and we must ring your friends there and warn them when we'll be flying out! — Ricco, won't they be thrilled to see us? . . . '

To see US. I walked away, the phrase like a knife turning in my mind.

Another voice challenged me, 'Keep smiling, it may never happen!'

I muttered, 'I think — I'm afraid — it's happening already, Alex.'

If he had seen how Abigail's casual words wounded me, it couldn't be helped. I saw there was strain written into his face too as he looked after his brother. He said quietly, 'If I could magic all the clocks on a few hours, I'd be a happier bunny. You don't know any spells?'

'Sorry. If I did. I've have used them. But — aren't we all getting things out of proportion over this concert today? — after all,' I protested in very forced reassurance, 'it's just a hyped-up kids' show, no more than that! Surely Sammy's right, he can do it with his eyes shut?'

If I were trying to convince myself as well, the attempt failed equally with us both. Alex said soberly, 'I'm not so sure he can. Rachel, did you know — the last time my brother played in public was the day Tina was found drowned in the lake?'

The stark words were totally unexpected. In the heat of the sunshine I was chilled through. I whispered,

'That's — horrible!'

'It is. And it gets worse. Do you want to know the rest?'

At last, at long last, it seemed he had been moved to fill in the gaps in the tale half-told the first time we took the children for a beach picnic. Perhaps he felt I was so deeply involved now that I should know the rest. Or perhaps he just needed to talk about it to someone.

We were sitting together now on the stone verge of the lily-pool. Two pink blooms rested their petals on the water. But water wasn't always so tranquil and innocent.

'You know I once told you, the day she died they quarrelled? It was a more than usually violent quarrel. Rick thought she was — seeing someone else . . . he was seen by more than one witness at the hotel shaking her in one of his mad rages — shouting at her to tell the truth, forbidding her to go out, threatening her . . . And that's why for a while he was accused of causing her death. Of — killing her.'

I made a wordless sound. The low-voiced story went relentlessly on.

Christina was a lovely, active girl — a beautiful dancer, a strong and fearless swimmer. She swam every day. That fateful day that was to be her last was very hot, with dramatic storm-clouds matching the flashpoint between the sadly warring Corellis. Tina must have suffered one of her occasional severe headaches because of the traumatic quarrel and the heat: she could have taken too much of her medicine, or in confusion she took it twice over. As a result, when she obstinately went out swimming to show Rick he hadn't won, she lost consciousness in the water and drowned.

For a moment Alex's voice wavered. He turned his head away from me.

'When she didn't come in later. Rick thought she'd walked out on him — if he thought at all. It wouldn't have been the first time. He didn't report her missing. The next day he was giving a recital, playing as brilliantly as ever, just going on with his life . . . and the police came to the concert hall, they told him Tina had — had been found in the lake . . . '

'Alex. He didn't — he *wouldn't* — would he? How could anyone think — ?'

Mutely, Rick's brother shook his head. It was a moment before he could find more words.

'He went through a bad time, a lot of intensive questioning. In the end there wasn't enough real evidence to make any charges stick. But the shock of that as well as Tina's death, it was too much, it — it just blew his mind. His memory blanked completely, for a while he didn't know who he was, where he was — let alone whether or not he'd really given his wife a deliberate overdose! . . . Rachel, I honestly believe he's still not sure about that even now . . . '

I felt sick. He put a gentle hand on my arm.

'I'm sorry. I'm sorry to have to tell you — '

'Please.' I whispered, 'I have to know all of it.'

There wasn't much more he could tell me. Only that Rick's stunned family managed to keep the publicity to a minimum, and took him to the Bergmann Clinic in Switzerland — run by a man he had known for some years as a friend but whose professional help was needed. Rick apparently made a reasonable recovery. He returned 'home' to his Uncle Cesare's — and this summer, as I knew, moved back to England. Carl Bergmann had encouraged him to start on the therapeutic task of writing his memoirs.

But lately Rick seemed to have suffered occasional memory lapses and disturbing 'flash-backs': indeed, had I not witnessed some of those myself, when some trifling cause sparked off a strange reaction? Had I not seen a sudden thunder-clap bring him visions of another stormy sky, of a defiant young swimmer who didn't return? . . .

I couldn't ask Alex about that final sad quarrel, whether poor Christina was indeed 'seeing someone else' — and whether he himself was that 'someone'. It was yesterday's tragedy. Today mattered now much more.

'I believe it's getting worse,' he was saying. 'I'm just not sure what this public performance will do to him.'

'We've got to stop it happening! If we can get hold of this man Bergmann? — '

'I've tried and tried. He's away on vacation. Boating — fishing — I don't know.'

'Why did you let it all go so far?' I flared at him, and then quickly amended that. 'No, I'm sorry — if it's anyone's fault it's mine. My Aunt warned me something was wrong. I didn't want to listen to her . . . '

There I stopped short, we both looked round. Rick and Abigail were already leaving. It was Abbey who backed out Rick's car with careless competence.

From the house Georgie was waving and calling out, 'Absolutely super luck, Ricky! — we'll try to be in the front row!'

I glimpsed Mrs. Nicholson beside her. The family audience didn't help, but somehow I started forward, planting myself directly in the path of the car.

'Excuse me! Abigail, before you go — we have to talk to you!'

'Can't stop. We're behind time. Will you move out of the way?' she requested impatiently.

'It's very important! It has to be *now* — '

Her response was simply to set the car moving. Both Alex and I skipped smartly aside.

'Later, all right?' Abigail called back to us over one azure-blue shoulder.

It wasn't all right. 'Later' could be too late.

* * *

I had a dull and constant feeling of apprehension when presently I arrived for the second time at the school. Now it was in Alex's car, and Mrs. Nicholson was next to him with her leg supported by cushions: we had both suggested she stayed home, and both been suitably and soundly quashed. I shared the back seat with Georgie, attired in one of her strange black concoctions with bead earrings resembling bell-pulls.

We found The Heights buzzing, not just with its cheery balloons and streamers but all the visitors who had arrived during the morning to view the displays and sample refreshments in the striped marquee. Clearly they weren't all families and friends: Abigail had done a good publicity job — so there were press photographers with lenses poised waiting at vantage points, a murmuring crowd already filling what proved to be a large modern hall. I gave Alex a glance of dismay, and he looked back at me equally grimly.

Evidently we were guests of honour, because a harrassed junior teacher pounced on us to enquire, 'Mrs. Nicholson's party? — yes, Miss Jesmond specially reserved your seats, can I show you? . . . '

It was nothing like those famous concert venues I had been typing about all these weeks, just a particularly opulent and spacious school hall . . . but visible through half-open curtains was the piano in solitary state at one side of the platform. I thought the beating of my heart must sound above the expectant hum all around.

To Georgie's satisfaction our seats were right in the front, with even a footstool provided for Mrs. Nicholson. Georgie was on one side of her. Alex on the other, propping a cushion behind her back. I sat next to him, very close to him.

Promptly on time, a quite composed Miss Jesmond appeared between the curtains to welcome everyone to this year's Music Festival. Due to the illness of her Head of Music, and a last-minute disaster befalling her Deputy, there had been 'wailing and gnashing of teeth', she told us with her pleasant smile — but a 'happy reprieve' enabled her to announce that today's programme *would* proceed as planned.

It did proceed, as listed in our stylish photocopied leaflets — a surprisingly ambitious and accomplished programme: the Upper School Choir, the Junior Recorder Group. Melissa Standish singing 'Amazing Grace', Hayley Beckham's somewhat squeaky violin solo — and so on, and so on. Rick had slipped unobtrusively into his place, and that daunting sheaf of sheet-music with pencilled directions was being steadily diminished piece by piece. I saw his face in profile, slightly frowning, intently watchful of the performers. I saw his hands moving easily over the keys.

Miss Jesmond hadn't named names, but it seemed as though everyone knew. Heads were craning. My heart was still racing, every minute seemed an hour. Only vaguely I realised I was clinging fast to Alex's hand . . . still more tightly when the cheery Miss Carstairs, acting as 'MC', introduced the next item: 'A piano solo from Samantha Thornton, a very talented young lady who hasn't been here long but we were so impressed with her we just had to squeeze her into the programme! . . . '

Alex breathed in my ear. 'You know what they say — 'It'll be All Right on the Night'.'

'But *all* these people . . . suppose she just curls up!'

Sam didn't curl up. I saw Rick relinquish his place to her with a little reassuring pat on her shoulder, with even a glimpse of his unforgettable dimpled smile. Guiltily I felt my mind had been so occupied with him I had almost overlooked Sam's big moment: but now, I listened as she wobbled just a little at the start but soon lost her nervousness in the beauty of the music. It was a performance not merely note perfect but deeply sensitive. She finished triumphantly, beaming up at Rick, smiling shyly towards the audience with glimmering glasses.

After Sam we had more singing, and then Mariella Bourne's ballet display. Again I saw Rick concentrating, intently following the accomplished young dancer.

This was the last item before the interval. There was a hum of chatter as people drifted from their seats to get cool drinks, fanning themselves with their programmes in the oppressive heat. Through the open doors were visible banks of black cloud spreading ominously across the heavy sky. Only another hour to sit here imagining horror on horror. One more hour before we could be away from here and the nameless danger would be over . . .

Alex was trying to settle Mrs. Nicholson more comfortably. I glimpsed

Abigail talking importantly to people at the back of the hall. Georgina gave me her patronising judgment. 'Not bad for a kids' show . . . but they'd never have got through it without Ricky, he's a Real Trouper.'

She was right about that. Bar a minor hitch or two with timing, a few visible signals exchanged between the 'MC' and the accompanist, everything flowed along — singing, instrumental solos, the short musical drama about that ever ubiquitous 'Lady of St. Denna' (the twins not helping it by making faces across at their father) — all building up to a grand finale with the whole company of performers packing the stage for 'Jerusalem'. That was moving enough to bring the house down.

A flushed and relieved Miss Jesmond took centre stage again for her closing speech. thanking participants and audience. But she had more than that to say.

'You'll all have realised the very vital role of our accompanist in holding the programme together . . . and our accompanist today provided his time and expertise in a major crisis with *no* prior notice . . . he wanted to remain anonymous, but I'm sure you all know who he is! So, ladies and gentlemen, I have the honour to thank Riccardo Corelli on behalf of the school and everyone present — and I know you'll agree the best way of thanking him is to ask him to play for us — this time not just background music but something of his own choice! . . .'

Again I gripped Alex's hand. The piano was moved to centre prominence. On the platform the throng of children were grouped around — Jade and Jenna I saw, glowing now with pride. Camera bulbs flashed in the gloom of the hall.

Perhaps it was strange that for all my years of admiration for the musician, for these weeks of growing closeness to the man, in all that time I had never seen him play as he could play. Now I saw, and now I heard. He gave a little resigned nod to Miss Jesmond, he sat again at the keyboard. There was pattering rain on the roof of the hall, but it was lost in the ethereal ripples of Chopin mounting gradually to a tragic passionate splendour of sound. The gift he had, that nameless gift, poured forth all the joy he had known, all the grief he had suffered, into a tide of music soaring to the higher places of the soul.

There were tears running down my face. Enraptured with beauty, I forgot the fear and anxiety of here and now, the threat of urgent danger. All was forgotten — until a vivid lightning flash shimmered eerily around the walls, until the lowering sky erupted into a great fusillade of thunder.

The music died on a gross discord. The pianist jumped to his feet and for one moment stood as though transfixed, his face pale and wild.

What happened next was a swift-moving dream. I heard my own voice cry out, 'Rick!' — and I was pushing my way desperately towards the lighted stage, falling over feet, shoving aside the startled ranks of children. But I was too late to reach him. Somehow he was down from the platform, making a dive for the nearest exit door.

The amazed audience were a vague sea of faces as I chased past them, still shoving aside shocked people who had no idea what was happening. But I knew. Dear heaven, I knew! — that Rick was trying to flee from a vision of the past he had not dared remember. Today, here in the public gaze, that cruel memory had finally come back to him.

I went on running, calling his name. Outside the hall it was almost like night. I saw the ceiling of black dramatic cloud, the eerie flickers of lightning. I felt the rain drenching my hair, my light dress clinging round my legs.

Among all the other parked vehicles clustered in the deluge, Rick's white car stood out. With eyes half blinded by water I saw him scramble into it — and close behind me now were other hurrying people. I heard the twins screaming, 'Daddy, what's wrong? — Daddy, wait for us!' I thought I heard Abigail's voice shouting, and Alex's.

Rick couldn't have heard any of us. He wouldn't have waited. The car shot forward at a crazy speed, its headlights suddenly piercing the gloom. There were other people spilling out of the hall, a confusion of voices.

'Daddy!' Jade and Jenna were still shrieking.

I screamed too, trying to stop the two girls in their frantic rush through the puddles. Hand in hand, they reached the entrance drive as the car swung round on to it. They were running directly into its path.

All I could do was make one wild dive to drag the children clear. In that same second I was aware the driver took violent evasive action, skidding the car halfway up a steep grassy bank, fighting for control.

I lay on the streaming roadway, breathless and bruised, the two girls in my arms. There was a frightening squeal of brakes. The sliding, hurtling vehicle skidded past us, completely misjudging the slope, the turn of the drive, the brick wall and iron gates.

In a melee of water and crunching glass and metal, the car turned right over.

* * *

I was huddled on a big settee in an unfamiliar sitting-room, in a borrowed dressing-gown and an enveloping blanket.

There was a smear of blood on my hands and knees. I felt battered and bruised. Still lightning flickered at the window, still rain pelted. In two more enveloping blankets, Jade and Jenna were close beside me, pale-faced, damp-haired, holding tightly to me.

'A marvellous escape,' someone was saying. Someone else said, 'A terrible tragedy.' Hands were offering hot drinks. I didn't know who all the people were. I kept asking for Sam, but no-one seemed to answer. Then an authoritative figure was taking charge, creating order. She was Sister Rylance, tall, brisk of manner, who looked after the First Aid and Sick-Room facilities at The Heights. We were in Miss Jesmond's house adjoining the school, she explained. We were all quite safe, just drenched and bruised — but obviously we should be checked over at the Hospital.

I felt the twins' quiver of dissent and said, 'Later. Maybe later. Please tell me . . . '

In very restrained fashion, in the children's presence, she told me that Riccardo Corelli was still being extricated from the wrecked car: that an ambulance was standing ready, his brother was with him and a young blonde woman, Miss Somebody.

'Horton,' I supplied.

'That's right. She's doing an excellent

job out there. Calming people down, dealing with the press, the police, everyone else! . . . '

'She would,' I had to agree.

In fact, in only a few moments Abigail looked round the door, holding an ashen-faced Sam by the hand. She told her kindly, 'There you are, Sammy, there's your sister — you stick by her, she's going to need you! . . . Rachel, are you all right?'

Her sunshine hair hung round her face in dripping strands. Someone's crumpled mackintosh was clutched around the ruin of the floaty blue dress.

'We're fine. Thanks, we're all fine. Abbey,' I blurted out, 'have you seen — ?'

'I really can't tell you much, but they just got him into the ambulance — they said he was half-conscious now, that's got to be a good sign!' She came over to me and gave an encouraging touch to my arm. 'He's in good hands, I promise. You stay here with the kids.

There's absolutely nothing you can do out there.'

There *was* something I could do. I could be near him. I could touch him, speak to him, I could suffer with him . . .

She told me briskly, Alex and Mrs. Nicholson were going straight along to the Penmoryn Hospital. I objected, 'Surely not Mrs. Nicholson? — she's still an invalid herself!'

'Not any more, she's not. She's sitting in Alex's car waiting for the off. She's a tough old — ' She coughed and amended. 'She's a very tough lady. She told me to say hallo and a huge thank-you — and she'll let you know as soon as there's some news.'

I nodded mutely. Jade and Jenna snuggled still closer to me.

'Gotta go!' Abigail was already turning back to the door and the rain. 'I've lots of loose ends to tie up out there — then I'll go on to the Hospital, I want to be there when poor darling Ricco wakes up . . . Look, if you get calls back at Gull Cliff you don't want — the press or whoever — give them my mobile number or say I'll ring back, okay?'

Again, I nodded. It was only then I realised she was shivering. I urged, 'Abbey, there's some hot tea here . . .'

'Can't stop. See you later, right? . . . And — you did a super thing out there, Ray.'

It was the first time she had called me that. Maybe the first time I had called her 'Abbey', that I had felt for her anything other than huge resentment. And the resentment was still there — because she was on her way to the bedside of her 'darling Ricco' . . .

I wanted to ask her, 'Give him my dearest love.' I couldn't say that, of course. If I said it, would the message ever reach him?

Sister Rylance had hurried off to deal with some of the shocked pupils, but someone else stayed with us. A little later a car had been arranged to transport the children and me — and

Georgina, rounded up from somewhere after 'having silly hysterics all over the place.' Sam whispered to me — back to the empty walls of Gull Cliff. Everyone was very kind, engulfing us in offers of help. A deeply distressed Miss Jesmond hovered over our departure, offering to send someone home with us, or even to let us stay where we were overnight. I told her I had to get the children home.

When at last we went out to the taxi, the storm had passed and there were spreading fragments of blue sky. Most of the visitors had left, but a few people were still talking in sober groups. My blood chilled as I saw the wreckage of the car, cordoned off with plastic tapes. I tried to keep the twins from staring at it.

Miss Jesmond, solicitously helping us along, murmured to me, 'You know. Miss Thornton, I still don't understand why . . . '

'He had a big problem with thunderstorms. Because of something that once happened to him. He hasn't been well ever since.'

'I know he was ill, but I wish Iris had told me more about it. I shall always blame myself for — '

'You mustn't. It was no-one's fault. It — just had to happen sometime.'

The twins sobbed their way through the short drive. Georgina didn't help by joining in. Sam sat straight and still and silent.

By the time we reached Gull Cliff, the house was bathed in golden evening sunshine. There was the scent of rain-drenched flowers. I thought absurdly, Alex wouldn't need to hose them to-night.

For a while, there were purely practical things to do. I got Georgina to stir herself and make us some sort of supper. I persuaded Jade and Jenna into a warm bubble-bath. Finally, all of us were in the big handsome lounge, waiting and waiting for the phone to ring. I set an example by nibbling some toast that almost choked me. The electric fire flickered its imitation embers gently in the hearth. The gull-chorus went on above the cliffs as though the world were unchanged.

No-one thought of going to bed. Finally, the warmth and quiet made the twins' eyelids droop. They were barely disturbed by several assorted phone enquiries and messages — but instantly awake again when the call came through from Alex at the Hospital.

My heart lurched in a relief beyond describing to hear that his brother was to undergo an urgent operation but his life was in no immediate danger. But the news wasn't really good. For a brilliant professional pianist it wasn't. There were head and other injuries still to be properly assessed — but it seemed Rick's right arm and *especially his hand* had been very severely damaged.

'I'll bring Gran home a bit later,' Alex said. 'She's amazing, sitting in the waiting-room like Mother Courage. There's one little nurse here already had to tidy her hair and tie up her shoe-laces.'

He said that with some attempt at the usual lightness in his low pleasant voice. In fact, he sounded near to tears.

'I can imagine. Look after her,' I said shakily. 'And, Alex — look after yourself, yes?'

To him, no more than to Abigail, could I confide my longing aching message, 'And give Rick my very dearest deepest love for always.'

For Rick's waiting family I paraphrased what I had learnt. Their Daddy was very ill at present but he would be better in a while. I assured the twins. The nature of his injuries turned Sam's pale face a few shades whiter. It was Georgie, of course, who breathed soulfully, 'Oh, isn't it *just* like in the films? — the world-famous musician who Can't Ever Play Another Note?'

I snapped at the girl, maybe unfairly, 'Well, it's NOT a film is it? It may be a wonderful piece of drama for you, but for him it's real!'

In any case, these days doctors and surgeons could perform near miracles. They might even piece together a crushed and mangled hand. I hastened to stress that mainly for the benefit of my stricken sister.

The time went on passing slowly, and eventually Georgie dozed, curled up under a blanket. The twins were determined to stay awake now, 'Just in case Daddy comes home to bed' — and I couldn't disillusion them. It was Sam who sat close to them on the sofa and gently tried to comfort them.

'He *will* be all right. You'll see. And he won't want us worrying ourselves sick, he won't want to hear we're sitting around crying, will he?' Her own eyes were dry, dark-shadowed behind those studious glasses that no-one laughed at tonight. Very kindly she was smoothing back Jenna's tangled hair, mopping up Jade's tear-streaked face.

Only a few minutes later, she had

fallen asleep. For my Sammy, this had been an interminable day. Before the moment of shocking tragedy struck, there was all the tension and triumph of her own performance. I reflected sadly, fondly, that the painfully withdrawn young sister I brought here to Cornwall had today shown her true worth.

And it seemed some such thought had come too to Jade and Jenna, who in past days had done their best to make Sam's life a burden to her. They were whispering together unintelligibly. It was Jade who finally spoke up in tremulous English, still half defiant.

'She's nice. She keeps on being nice to us. And — we did this really mean and horrible thing — she'd hate us if she knew, and — you'd hate us too, and Great-Gran would *kill* us! — '

I offered softly, 'Do you want to tell me? Would it help?'

They wriggled unhappily. This time it was Jenna who found the words.

'Great-Gran's things. We took them!'

'You took — ?'

'Her money. And her brooch thing out of the box. And — we meant to put it in Sam's school-bag or somewhere so she'd get in awful trouble —'

'Yes, 'cos our Daddy kept on taking for ever and ever teaching her the piano,' Jade took up the tale. 'We thought it wasn't fair! So — so — '

'So we did it,' her twin confessed. 'And then Liz got sent away, and we got scared, and — we didn't dare own up! And now you know, and you'll tell Great-Gran, and — *will* she get us sent to prison for stealing?'

For immediate answer, I opened my arms. Suddenly they were filled with a tangle of warm bodies, clinging hands, tearful faces, the two little girls whose brief lives had held too fast a whirl of excitements, too deep a well of sorrow and loss. Through all these weeks I had tried and failed to get close to Rick's motherless children. It had taken the shock of today to let me reach them.

I held them close and promised to help them tell their Great-Gran and give her property back — she would forgive them, and Sam need never know. They snuggled up to me, snuffling, rubbing their heavy eyes. It wasn't long before both were breathing deeply and peacefully, forgetting in sleep their wrongs and regrets, whatever changes today might make to their lives.

Alone in the silent slumbering room my eyes were still wakeful. I dared not move for fear of disturbing the girls. I watched the summer darkness at the window, the hands of the clock creeping towards midnight.

It was past that when headlights reflected in the gloom as Alex's car drew to a halt. No-one in the room woke. I slipped away to greet the arrivals: his face looked haggard as he helped his Grandmother into the house. Limping bravely on, she made a good attempt at her usual brisk manner.

'Well, Rachel, here we are, my dear! . . . The end of a chapter, I'm afraid.

Today we've probably witnessed the *last* performance Ricky Corelli will ever give. And heaven help him — and us! — when he realises.'

She didn't say much else. She let me help her to her room, to lie down fully clothed — 'In case we're called out, Abigail is staying with him and she'll ring if we're needed.'

Alex lifted the sleeping twins into their beds. I led a dazed and bleary Sam to hers, huddling the covers around her.

On the landing, Alex stood silently waiting. Utterly weary, for a moment I fell into his sustaining arms as the twins had fallen into mine.

'Come on, Rachel. Don't give up. There's always hope . . . for some among us,' he added softly.

I couldn't tell him — but I believed he knew — that some of my pain was because the vigil kept near Rick's bedside tonight was Abigail's. Abigail's, and not mine.

6

In the time that followed, Gull Cliff was a major hive of industry, abuzz with letters and phone messages, a confusion of comings and goings.

When I rang a horrified Doreen and Dawn, mercifully I was able to report, 'He did recognise his Gran — and Abigail . . . Alex took me to see him for just a moment but he didn't really know we were there . . .'

I didn't give full details of the accident, just that Rick had felt unwell during the concert and left early, and crashed his car in the blinding rain. That was the public version. Whatever Doreen thought privately, she kept it to herself in the face of my distress. Dawn wanted to know where to send cards and flowers, and said unsteadily, 'I just can't bear to think of it, he was — so lovely to look at . . .'

I whispered, 'He still is, Dawn. He still is.'

Their 'get well' cards arrived quickly. Just two among a large quantity of flowers and mail pouring in, from locals shocked by banner headlines in 'The Penmoryn Clarion', from the many people who knew Rick far and wide during his years of performing, or simply from 'fans' who had queued for his concerts. The accident received quite wide publicity in the national media. I knew Abigail had encouraged that, in some way looking shrewdly forward to the future. I supposed she knew what she was doing.

Certainly, she was managing all the business side of things very efficiently. But I had to bite my tongue hard at the imperious way she dealt with each day's letters: 'All these, just send the usual acknowledgements and thanks, Rachel! . . . I'll drop a line personally to this guy . . . send this old duck one of the signed photos . . . ' I hadn't come to Gull Cliff to be Miss Horton's secretary. In the circumstances, I could hardly protest.

The flowers posed more of a problem. Apparently Rick, as he became more aware of things, didn't want them — which sounded like Rick being Rick, maybe a hopeful sign? Abigail distributed them round the Hospital, and I sent out messages of thanks.

Then there were the visitors. One of the first was Carl Bergmann, who turned out to be a stoop-shouldered balding little man with gold-rimmed glasses. I felt like telling him he had arrived on the scene far too late — and evidently Alex did tell him just that, very forcibly, because I overheard heated voices. I was discovering that mild Alex could turn quite unexpectedly into fiery Alessandro, with a full share of the Corelli temperament.

Another of our visitors was an eminent and unpronounceable Hungarian conductor, whose English was appalling but whose kind concern was great: we treated him with awed reverence. There was also an influx of what Alex referred to as 'the Italian Corellis', Uncle Cesare and Aunt Francesca and assorted family on flying visits. The twins were thrilled to see them. Abigail, who of course had stayed with them a while back, greeted them like lifelong friends and took them under her wing. I thought from afar that Cesare was charming, and his daughter Renata had a dark dimpled smile reminding me achingly of Rick.

But I didn't see too much of any of them socially. Someone had to cook their meals and organise their rooms. I wondered what Liz Banner would have thought of the bulging household — and no assistance from 'Lady Muck' Georgina. It was touching that a few lines did come from Liz, on holiday with her Stevie in Torquay, that she was 'ever so sorry about the accident.' She added gleefully that she was getting engaged. Maybe, indeed, the twins had done her a favour: Alex and I sent her our private congratulations — and mentioned that the lost valuables had 'come to light'.

For a day or two the children stayed home from school, but then they returned to The Heights to finish out the term — only a matter of days, but 'far the best thing to keep them out of mischief,' Mrs. Nicholson decreed.

It shook me badly, the first day I took them, to see the area around the damaged gateway — and to live again the rain, the fear, the agony. The cheery Miss Carstairs, today very sober and serious, insisted she mustn't let me leave without seeing Miss Jesmond, on strict instructions: so I spent a half-hour sitting by the big desk where Sam had spoken up so bravely at her first interview — it seemed an age ago.

'Is it really true,' Miss Jesmond asked me with great distress, 'that he won't be able to — that he might not — '

'It's true. He's recovering . . . but some sorts of injury just aren't mendable. He's moving on to the Park Memorial

Hospital — near Exeter. They have special facilities, he'll have another operation, but . . . '

'Doctors and their opinions aren't infallible. Even the best of them — are they, Rachel?'

'No. And of course, he can try all the top specialists,' I said just to please her. We both of us knew that an irreversible injury was for life — and a pianist's cruelly crushed hand was bereft of its magic.

She gave me various kind messages for Mrs. Nicholson. As I left, her last words were simple and sincere: 'I feel very privileged to have been present at his last performance.'

I guessed that the children would be treated very gently for their remaining school days. Sam seemed to have withdrawn again behind her barrier of reserve. The twins were utterly subdued, and both wept in my arms after they were taken to visit their father.

Abigail was always in and out of

the Hospital, and Mrs. Nicholson — having discarded her own invalid status overnight — spent many hours there. Mostly Alex drove her, and ferried other people around when needed. I gathered he didn't go in himself to see Rick. Of course, that would be because he feared to stir the old animosity between them and do his brother harm: surely not because, if Rick had regained all his past memory, Alex was *ashamed* now to face the man he had once cruelly deceived?

During this time Rick didn't ask for me, and I didn't see him. Partly that was because I was so constantly busy, mostly because he had other people there. It was enough to have glimpsed his face mercifully unmarked and unchanged, to think ahead. I sent him notes that didn't say much except that he was constantly in my thoughts and my prayers. Mrs. Nicholson willingly delivered them, and assured me, 'He said thank you, he's very, very grateful to you for looking after the children and keeping the household going — and so am I, my dear. So am I.'

Which was nice, but I didn't want their gratitude. I wanted only to be with Rick again. Just to be with him, he and I alone.

'I must say,' his Grandmother said as well, 'he's dealing wonderfully well with the shock of what's happened. He's quite placid, you know. He's even being polite to everyone! — well, nearly everyone. He's very quiet, very *resigned* . . . '

Georgie murmured something about Bravery Beyond the Call of Duty. Alex marvelled, 'Placid? — resigned and polite? Gran, are you sure you're visiting the right patient?'

As she shook her head at him severely, he glanced at me and closed one blue eye. They weren't the same smiling eyes I had known during my first uncertain days among strangers at Gull Cliff. He didn't ever say much to me about his brother. He never tried to tell me again that he cared for me. When I needed him, he was always there.

With the school term ended, it was important to keep the children busy, with beach or cinema or shopping trips, with games, walks, videos. Georgina was very occasionally helpful, but these days I had no qualms about taking Jade and Jenna around unsupported. Certainly they hadn't become angels overnight, but mostly they were manageable. Sam still spent time at the piano — Rick had given instructions she could continue using it — but nowadays she stole guiltily into the music-room. I could understand that.

Abigail, tirelessly in and out of the house, the Hospital, or shooting off to 'meetings' or 'to visit contacts' (whatever that meant) had actually left us to stay a couple of days in London when Mrs. Nicholson arrived home late from a Wednesday afternoon visit. She almost bounced out of Alex's car.

'Rachel! Some very good news! Rick

will be coming home on Friday — how about that?'

I wondered if my face betrayed my feelings. I said just, 'This Friday?'

'This Friday! Only temporarily until he has more treatment — but meantime he'll be back with us again — so we must get his room all ready! Isn't that wonderful news?'

I said, 'It is. Yes, it is.'

I couldn't tell her that *wonderful* was a word totally inadequate.

* * *

All day Thursday it poured with rain. I set the cooped-up children to making a 'Welcome Home' banner, and Georgie supervised them grudgingly. I vacuumed Rick's room and supplied it with fresh flowers. It was a surprisingly frugal room, I always thought: books, a modest hi-fi system and stacks of recordings, but no family photographs or mementos. The windows looked out to sea, today grey and sullen tipped with galloping white horses.

The following morning was equally grey, with almost a hint of early Autumn in the air. Alex started out with his Grandmother shortly before eleven — and the major problem, of course, was to stop the twins piling into the car too: they protested loudly, 'Why do we have to hang round the silly old house all day?'

'Because there won't be room in the car,' Alex said patiently. 'Your Daddy mustn't be squashed! And when he gets home, you must be very quiet. He's had a bad time. He still isn't properly well.'

They made rude faces at him. Their 'new leaf' (promised tearfully to Mrs. Nicholson in the wake of the 'missing valuables' affair) did on occasion turn itself back again.

To pass the time I took the three girls into St. Denna, to the cafe that served those 'yummy chips' the twins had demanded on my first disastrous day of taking care of them. So much had happened since that day. It seemed in another world.

Back at the house, Georgie had returned from shopping but all was still quiet. Jade and Jenna stationed themselves at a front window. Alike as two peas, they were wearing the pretty outfits brought back from Italy, with yellow velvet ribbons fastening their hair. Sam sat bolt-upright, freckled and frowning.

'They're coming!' Jenna yelled suddenly, with scant regard to Alex's prior instructions. 'They're here! And I can see — '

'There's Daddy!' her sister confirmed. 'And he doesn't look *any* different, does he?'

That was untrue, as I soon realised. Holding a twin firmly captive in either hand I went out to the courtyard — my mind transporting me back to the day of Rick's previous homecoming, my first glimpse of the man I came to work for — the man who had become my life. A mixture of charisma and frailty and arrogance, I had thought then. Today the frailty was most evident.

His face was worn, thinner and paler. The shadowed black eyes seemed in contrast even darker.

As Georgie ran forward officiously to help him from the car, I saw him shake her off with the quite mild protest. 'Thanks, I'm not quite helpless yet.'

The wriggling twins tore away from me then. Mrs. Nicholson warned them sternly. 'Now *steady*, you girls! — do you hear me?'

Their father stooped to kiss the two excited upturned faces. The familiar lock of dark hair flopped over his forehead. He pushed it back with his one mobile hand, and then his eyes met mine.

'Rachel. Hallo.'

'Hallo!' I whispered. It seemed too obvious to ask how he was, and yet unforgivable not to ask. 'I — I'm so glad to see you home. Are you — ?'

'I'm all right. What's left of me. Grazie.'

'Come along inside, everyone!' Mrs. Nicholson ordered. 'Rick, you must get in the house, it's quite chilly out here. Rachel will fetch you a warm drink.'

'Rachel looks tired. You've been overworking her, Gran.'

'No, indeed! I certainly haven't! But she's been a tower of strength to us all,' she said warmly. 'I can't say what a blessing it's been to have her here.'

He said, 'You don't need to tell me.' Again his eyes lingered on mine. I felt my face flaming: I thought everyone must hear the riotous pulsing of my heart.

In procession we went into the house, Alex and Georgie in the rear with Rick's luggage. In the hallway hung the twins' WELCOME HOME banner — and those framed Corelli concert posters seeming to flaunt themselves along their wall.

I had made prior preparations, so it was easy to complete a trolley-load of scones and cake and fruit, a bowl of jelly-trifle which showed ominous signs of subsidence in its foundations: I hoped Mrs. Nicholson wouldn't measure the distance between the cherries. In the big lounge I handed out cups and plates to people chatting in a distinctly strained fashion. Georgie didn't help by staring in morbid fascination at Rick: he was sitting passively where he had been placed, his right arm held in a sling made of a black silk scarf, the maimed hand hidden.

'Where's Sam?' he asked.

Jenna announced, 'She's hiding! She ran upstairs when you came, I saw!'

I volunteered to find her. It didn't take long. Sam was hovering just outside the door, but I had to propel her in as Rick called to her, 'Come on, won't you say hallo to me?'

She didn't say 'hallo'. Standing beside his chair, her face paler than his, the words she stammered out were repeated over and over: 'I'm ever so sorry — it was all my fault . . . I know it was my fault . . . '

'What was all your fault?'

She made a wild nervous gesture. 'The accident, of course! Because — if I hadn't got you into that stupid show it would never have happened!'

I realised suddenly how blind and foolish I had been not to realise the huge lonely burden of guilt, as well as grief, that my sister had carried around with her ever since that fateful day. I heard Rick telling her, 'You mustn't ever think that, Sam. It was — an accident waiting to happen, not your fault at all. Yes? . . . And in the concert you played so well. So very well, I was proud to hear you.'

'Were you really?' she whispered.

'Have you been working well since? Did you get the better of that Study yet?'

'N-no. I still get stuck with the *agitato* part.'

'That won't do. That's bad! Come on, will you let me hear it?' he invited.

'You — you want me to play it? You mean — now?'

'Why not? We'll put it right — si?'

'Si!' Sam echoed. There was alarm and joy and relief strangely mixed in her face.

They went together towards the music-room, still deep in discussing their *rallentandos* and their *sempre legatissimos*. I tried to say, 'Sam, don't!' but the words froze on my lips. Mrs. Nicholson put out a restraining hand and drew it back. Both of us, as though drawn by an irresistible magnet, followed on.

Through the open doorway we saw the shining bulk of the instrument, the glimmer of its white keys. Sam was visibly shaking as she tried to play, muffing the first bars horribly. Rick encouraged her again, 'Gently . . . softly . . . let it sing to you . . . now the fire starts! No. like this, Sammy . . .'

Then, he was sitting beside her. His one mobile hand moved in illustration over the keys.

I heard Mrs. Nicholson mutter, 'Heaven save us.' I looked round and saw the tears bright in her eyes, spilling down her face. It was the only time ever I saw that.

The broken snatches of melody went on for a while. Not for too long. I was still piling up the used crockery when Sam sidled back in and beat Jenna to the last slice of cake. She announced, 'Rick's gone upstairs to rest. He said to tell you he's all right, just a bit tired.'

'Well, of course he is,' Mrs. Nicholson said too briskly, too loudly. 'It's been a very tiring day for him. He just needs time to get his strength back.'

She looked as though her own strength had deserted her, subsiding on to the sofa. Alex went quietly over to sit beside her.

There were the usual mundane things to do, and I did them, striving not to clash dish against dish. It seemed a premature dusk was falling, an early foretaste of autumn soon to come. Outside was heavy gloom, inside an eerie quiet. These enclosing walls were haunted by the glory of music they had once known and now was silenced . . . as though no-one dared make a sound, as though we were all waiting and waiting. For what were we waiting? . . .

At length the twins hunched sulkily beside Georgie over the television, tuned down lower than they liked: this homecoming evidently wasn't at all what they had hoped for. Mrs. Nicholson had actually fallen asleep. Alex passed me in the hall, on his way to the stairs.

'I'll just see if Rick's all right.'

I wanted to beg, 'Let me!' — but instead I just followed on at a distance. I heard a soft tap on Rick's door — and a sudden low-voiced exclamation. Then I was running and stumbling up the stairs.

'He's not there,' Alex said.

The room was empty, the bed crumpled as though from someone lying upon it restlessly. The black scarf lay discarded on the carpet.

It took us only a few moments to discover that Rick wasn't in any of the other rooms. He wasn't in the house at all — but the patio doors were ajar.

'He must have crept out without us hearing — but he can't have gone far, he's not strong enough! Alex, if he just wanted some air he'll be in the garden, won't he?'

'That's right, we'll soon find him. Don't alarm the others,' Alex said quickly, 'especially Gran — I'm not sure she can take much more.'

Outside it wasn't cold, just very gloomy, a strong breeze lifting my hair. All was emptiness. The pink water-lilies smiled in their pool. Stone urns of trailing white flowers were almost luminous.

'Could he have gone down the lane? — towards the village?'

'Maybe he has. I'll find him.' Alex squeezed my arm. 'Just stay here, keep a look-out in case he comes back.'

I watched his tall figure start off at a run. It was only a moment after he was gone that tardy inspiration came to me. No, Rick wouldn't go to the village — what reason would he have? There was somewhere else he would choose to go, a lonely place that I knew had a sombre fascination for him. Often I had seen him slip away down the rough steps to spend a few moments on that little hidden beach . . . perhaps because Tina had so loved that wild spot, perhaps simply to think of the girl whose last living moments were wide sky and engulfing water.

A great horror was growing now in me. I ran and stumbled down the steps, clinging to the rail. The wind was strong, flapping my hair in my face. Through my mind kept on passing those absurdly dramatic words the twins rehearsed over and over for their play, suddenly changed from a foolish legend to a vision of stark reality:

'Her long hair looped with seaweed.
And icy cold her hand.

'Tis the Lady of St. Denna
Lying drowned upon the sand . . . '

He was down there on the rocky beach. He was lying very still, his face against the wet shingle. The relief of seeing the slightest movement, of hearing him sigh or sob, was beyond all describing.

In my love for him, in this his darkest of hours, all I could do was to share the agony of his soul . . . to hold him in my arms, to weep too for that loss irretrievable, the girl he had loved, the music that was his breath of life. With the lowering evening sky above us, with the breeze and the sand and the sea. I held him close to me. I grieved with him, I suffered with him.

And soon I realised he was responding to me, perhaps to the love outpoured in my touch. The one strong hand strained me closer. I heard his struggling words, 'Rachel . . . I frightened you, I'm sorry . . . '

'It's all right. It doesn't matter. I love

you, Rick. I love you . . . '

The words were carried away in the wash and hiss of the tide. I didn't know if he had heard them. His face was hidden against me, I felt him trembling, shivering. He pleaded like a child, 'Help me! — Help me, don't leave me!'

'I won't leave you. Not ever,' I gave my promise — and now there was joy shining through this present pain. 'Rick, darling — don't give up, there's still so much left in the world for you! We'll find it. I promise we will. We can do so much for Jade and Jenna — and Sammy — together we can! . . . I love you, I love you so much . . . '

It was a sound on the steps leading down the looming cliff that made me realise we were no longer alone. Rick's brother was standing quite near to us on the rough stairway. His eyes met mine in a strange mingling of relief and sorrow.

Over Rick's bowed dark head nestled against me, I mouthed the same words over and over: 'I'm sorry — I'm so very sorry.'

Alex nodded, just once. As quietly as he came, he climbed back up towards the house.

* * *

In the morning I woke late from an hour or two of heavy sleep. For an eternity before that I had tossed and turned through a welter of broken dreams.

Was it just one of those dreams that last night I held Rick close to me on the wild shore — that we had wept and talked, heedless of the evening chill, the cold sea-spray, the screaming sea-birds? So many things he poured out to me, because the blank spaces in his mind were filled: he remembered and relived the day Christina died — and the doubts that had so long tortured him, whether or not in frenzied anger and jealousy he had really sent her to her death, were at last now laid to rest.

It *was* a cruel accident, no more. But it would be his eternal grief that their final parting was marred by discord and distrust.

'I ruined her life,' he kept saying. 'I loved her, but I ruined her life . . . so what happened to me is a judgment, yes? This is true justice, yes? So no use to fight it! Tina is gone, the music is gone. All this I must live with . . . '

I couldn't change any of that. All I could do was tell him again and again, the two little girls who adored him, Tina's little girls, needed him so badly. The time ahead need be no barren waste. And there could even be all the joys and blessings of a second love, a life reborn.

Dreams, only dreams? And only a dream that when finally I persuaded him to let me help him back to the house — in the dim garden he held me and kissed me so warmly, so tenderly? . . .

No, none of them dreams! There were the shoes I had worn, parked on some paper, still caked with sand! There was my dress, damp and creased! I could still hear his voice. I could still feel him holding me, his lips so urgently seeking and claiming mine.

Now in a mad scramble I was up and dressed, disbelieving that I had slept through my morning chores and no-one had called me. Sam must have gone down a while ago. Her bed was covered neatly, with Dawn's little teddy sitting openly on the pillow because nobody teased her about that now.

This morning there was bright sunshine at the windows, matching the sunshine in my heart. Soon I was hurrying downstairs, eager only to see his face again, to be with him. If he had slept deeply too in his exhaustion, today he would be rested and renewed — today he would be able to lift his head and face up to the future! To face — *our* future? . . .

In the hall I heard his voice somewhere, talking on the telephone, quite bright and excited. I caught a word or two: 'Next month? — yes, that'll do, book the flights — I'm sure I shall be able to make that!'

Was he planning for us some wonderful renewing holiday? Was he taking me to visit the Corellis in Italy? Was there anywhere we couldn't go, anything in the world we couldn't do?

'Good morning!' I greeted brightly the assembly in the morning-room. 'I overslept, I'm so sorry!' I saw my accusing untouched place at the table, and another that was Rick's. 'Mrs. Nicholson, how is he today?' I asked her anxiously. 'He — went for a walk last night, he wasn't very well . . . '

'So I've been told. He's much better, I'm glad to say! He's talking to Abigail — she's already rung twice this morning!'

She herself looked much better too. Truly she was amazing, I thought, last night seeming to have finally crumpled beneath the weight of her years and woes, this morning quite her composed and capable self. She had evidently breakfasted Jenna and Jade and Sam, who were sitting in a subdued row washed and brushed.

'Jenna, don't scrape your feet on that chair,' her Great-Grandmother directed. 'Rachel, that toast will be stone cold, I should make some more. — Oh, there's a card for you, it came yesterday and got overlooked . . .'

Yesterday I hadn't worried about cards. Today as well, I gave scarcely a glance at the postcard by my plate: a London view, and on the reverse some lines in Aunt Doreen's no-nonsense writing. She and Greg had spent a few days with friends. Pa was doing nicely. No doubt Sam and I would be starting home shortly as they would vacate the house early in September.

I realised Mrs. Nicholson's searching eyes were turned sharply my way. My face flamed as I wondered exactly how much she knew of last night's proceedings — she had actually slept through my return from the beach with Rick. She was starting to pile up the breakfast plates with a brisk clatter. Georgina got up reluctantly to help. Alex was sitting by the window, as subdued as the children.

It was only a few moments later when Rick came into the room. My heart lurched all anew as I looked into his face, that dark so-familiar face — today very far from a face of despair.

'Well, Ricky, what's the answer?' Mrs. Nicholson asked him, with bright eagerness. His nod of assent seemed to excite her even more. 'She really thinks she can fix things up? — that's wonderful! I may have said a few things about Abigail in the past — hem! — but you've got to give the girl her due. She has what it takes in her line of business! She's a go-getter!'

He agreed quietly, 'She's more than that.'

'Rachel, you'll want to know what's going on.' his Grandmother swept on. 'Abbey has found this very exciting opening for Rick, it could be the start of a whole new career! A film to be made in Hollywood about a musician — they want some of Rick's recordings for the background, and he'll do some arrangements and be a sort of musical consultant — '

'Gran,' Alex tried quietly to interpose, 'it's not signed and sealed yet.'

'If Abbey says it can be fixed, I'm sure she's right. Did she give you any dates, Rick?'

'Next month. We'll fly out to meet the Director — if I'm well to go. And I shall be.'

'Of course you will be.' She put her hand fondly on his shoulder.

'There's also something else. She contacted this Dr. Van Driemer who has a Clinic in New York, he specialises in accident cases which leave bad disabilities. Abbey says he is very interested to try helping me . . . '

To that part of the sensational news I could scarcely give attention. Only one fact had penetrated my numbed mind. Just one. A new door had opened for Riccardo Corelli to go on living his interrupted life: in another form the broken melody would begin again — a wonder of wonders, a cause for rejoicing! But . . . he was flying out to the States for the new work, for the new medical treatment, for the whole blossoming new life — with Abigail Horton.

So finally, had Abbey won? For what could I offer him to compare with so much — except my dearest love for always?

My voice was as quiet and distant as his brother's as I said, 'I'm very happy for you, Rick. I hope it all works out.'

He had sat down now across the table from me. I saw instantly the transforming new life that had come to his face. I saw the glow lighting those tragic eyes.

He smiled across at me. Dear heaven, that smile.

'I'm sorry we won't finish the book, Rachel. But I never wanted to do it anyway — it was Carl's idea, not mine. He said it would be good for me. It *was* good, it brought you here to us for all this time . . .'

Don't smile at me, almost I cried aloud. How can I bear that smile?

'Of course, you'll have a very good bonus, for all your hard work. And I suppose anyway you'll want to get back to London very soon now? — Sam's school will have its new term starting?'

I couldn't answer him. My throat was choked and mute.

'And I must thank you for your help and understanding yesterday.' So close to me, that soft voice with its inflection of a foreign shore: so close, and an eternity away. 'I was very tired — very upset . . . I'm sorry about that, you were so kind and comforting. So very kind . . .'

I looked at him. Across the table with its yellow gingham cloth and a vase of yellow flowers, I looked into his eyes. Last night he had bared his soul to me. Last night our lips had met and lingered. Had it really meant so little to him?

Silently I sat there, a being of ice and stone and abiding hurt. Across a void there were other voices around me — an excited Georgie clamouring for details of the forthcoming film, the twins lamenting, 'Daddy, it's not fair! — you're just back home, and now are you going off and leaving us again? — '

'No, I'm not leaving you. This time you'll come too. Do you remember my friends Jo and Peg Schwartz, their big house with the huge blue swimming pool? — they have plenty of room for a while for Abbey and us! — '

'Yippee!' the girls yelled.

They bounced like demented jack-in-the-boxes, until their Great-Grandmother hushed them. 'We don't want all this noise, just simmer down! . . . Rick, if you want to get any strength back at all, you sit there and eat something! And — my dear, *don't* get your hopes up too high about this Dr. What's-his-Name, but — well, there's always hope!'

The same words Alex once said — and added, 'For some people, there is.'

By now I had glimpsed my sister's utterly devastated face. I grabbed up my London postcard, I slipped from my chair and out of the room.

After yesterday's greyness the morning was beautiful. Blue sky, blue sea, nodding flowers, the warmth of sunshine on my chilled skin. I didn't want to see the beauty all around, part of a dream that had lasted one long enchanted summer. I stood there like a stone.

It was a gentle hand on my arm that brought reality back to me. If there were warmth and comfort in that touch, it didn't reach me.

'I'm sorry,' Alex said. 'I'm so very sorry. I did try to warn you.'

'I love him. I thought — he loved me too. Yesterday . . . '

'I know. But that was yesterday. Now it's today — and with my brother other things get in the way of loving. This is Rick,' he said softly. 'All his heart and soul and life and love is in his music, and his music is magnificent — if he can find it again in some way that's wonderful! He's a brilliant musician but he just isn't such a brilliant human being . . . he hurts people badly, he doesn't realise how much he hurts them . . . '

Still he held me. I saw the pain in his face. I heard the shake in his voice.

'Rachel, what else can I say? I'm so sorry. I didn't want you hurt like Tina was hurt, I should have helped you more — '

'It doesn't matter now. And I wouldn't have listened to you.' I lifted my head suddenly. 'Anyway, it's ended! I've been given my orders to leave — and 'a bonus for all my kindness' . . . how could he *do* that, after we . . . ?'

Alex didn't speak. It was a question beyond all answering.

I lifted my head higher still, in

sudden resolution.

'Well, all right, I'll go home! Back home to my own little world! It's high time. And I've got to make it up to poor Sammy . . . ' The tears I wouldn't shed for myself welled now for my sister, blurring my view of the sunny garden, the blue-shuttered house, the tall quiet man beside me.

I broke away from him, and turned back quickly inside. I guessed Sam would have hidden away upstairs, and I found her face down on her bed: I sat close beside her, stroking her hair, saying what there was to say.

We had such lots to tell Pa, I kept repeating. We would buy exciting presents to take back for everyone. Miss Crocker would be so pleased to restart regular lessons — and delighted with the huge progress Sam had made.

'And, Sammy, I've been thinking — St. David's School, down the hill, has music scholarships. They're hard to get, but you'd stand a good chance! Suppose we put your name down?'

'I don't know,' she muttered. 'I thought I'd stay at The Heights. I like it there. I'm best friends with Mariella Bourne — '

'You can write to Mariella. Invite her to stay with us.'

'But I *like* it there . . . and I was sure we'd stay on at Gull Cliff.' She rolled round to look at me. 'I thought Pa could be somewhere much nearer, and I'd stay at the school, and — you'd marry Rick. Well,' she pointed out with half-accusing logic, 'when you came in with him last night I was watching, I saw the way he kissed you! — didn't he? And you kissed him back! And I really did think . . . '

So did I think, Sammy. So did I.

What I could do to comfort her. I did. It seemed to me, what we needed now, the pair of us, was *speed* — to get right away, to stay not one extra moment among our fragmented dreams. That same morning I sought out Mrs. Nicholson alone and handed over a formal typed letter.

‘Notice to leave?’ She glanced at the lines and then at me, her blue penetrating eyes deeply concerned. ‘Are you sure about this? Oh, I heard what Rick said about the book, but there’s no need at all for you to rush away!’

‘I think he’s right, I do need to go home. Sammy’s schooling, and my father . . . I don’t want to make things difficult for you, but as soon as I can be spared . . . ’

‘Well, let me see.’ She pondered, still frowning at the letter. ‘I believe the Bassetts are ready to come back to me. Alex has business in London to see about — but Georgie will stay till Rick and the girls leave. So really you can go when you like.’

‘Can I? If I ring my Aunt today — say tomorrow?’

‘Yes, tomorrow. If that’s what you want, Rachel. If you feel you must.’

There was sadness in her voice and her face — and as well, I thought, shrewd understanding in her eyes. I believed she knew exactly why I had to go. For her too, in all the thrill of her adored Rick's new hopes, this was one dream shattered.

She said abruptly, 'I shall be sorry to lose you. I hope you'll come down to visit me. When everyone's gone about their business, I'll be moping around like a lonely old woman.'

Never that, I wanted to tell her — but already she had turned away, as though fearing to say too much. By now I had my own feelings well in check. I couldn't let my resolution waver.

On that last Saturday — so unexpectedly the last — there was so much to do, so little time to do it. I took Sam off to Penmoryn for a shopping spree, lavishly buying presents. Then there was our hectic round of packing: we had accumulated double the goods and chattels we arrived with — or it seemed that way.

Deliberately I kept Sam busy, away from the rest of the household. We even excused ourselves from the evening meal, supplementing sandwiches upstairs: we were so busy, Sam had to get an early night ready for the journey. I put forward Sam's name, but in truth I couldn't face Rick across the table, listening to more of his plans. Or Miss Horton's plans.

When I rang Doreen she was understandably surprised, but delighted. We would have some nice days together before she and Greg went home. She would have everything ready for us, and tell Pa we were on our way.

Another beautiful late-summer morning, this last day dawned. There was no Sunday peace in the household. Everyone was astir early. I would far rather just have slipped away without a ritual of goodbyes.

The twins were quite affectingly upset to part with us, promising Sam they would write from the States. They clung to me limpet-like with copious tears. I believed, in the end, I really had got through to those troubled and defiant little girls. I wondered what sort of life lay ahead for them.

The car was already half-loaded, and the remaining bags and bundles were pushed in haphazardly. The gifts I had bought for Jade and Jenna I gave to their Great-Grandmother, to be opened presently. She was tut-tutting at me sternly because we were committing the crime of going off with no breakfast.

'We'll get something along the way. Sam can't eat anyway! I have to go.' I told her quite desperately now — and I knew she understood. Unexpectedly she held me in a very warm embrace. She whispered. 'I know you do . . . and I'm sorry.'

She would never let one word against Rick pass her lips, but I knew she was trying to apologise for a grievous case of heartache. Already she had handed me an envelope with the final cheque due to me, and an extra cheque signed by Rick which amounted to more than the whole summer's earnings: I had tried to return it, but she wouldn't hear of that: 'Put it aside for Samantha.

She's a good girl. Do that for me, Rachel.'

So the cheque was in my bag, and tomorrow it would be in the bank. For myself, I wouldn't touch a penny of it.

Sam was already waiting by the car. Alex waved from the doorway, and Georgie called a casual 'Bye!' It was only then that Rick came quietly over to us.

'Rachel, how can I say this? . . . I'm so very sorry to see you go. I'm sorry we couldn't finish the book. And thank you for helping Jade and Jenna so much. Thank you most of all for — putting up with me . . . '

He reached for my hand, and I fought a fierce inward fight against the touch of him, the nearness of him. His black vivid eyes looked once more into mine. The smile that had already broken my heart just wavered.

I said. 'I don't want any thanks. I just hope — things work out for you.'

They were the last words. I saw him

take my sister's hand too and speak to her softly. 'Keep working, Sammy. You'll get there. Si?'

She managed a choked 'Si!' and bundled in a heap into the car.

I had actually started it moving, against the background of waving hands, when Alex ran after us. He handed in a forgotten carrier-bag.

Totally beyond words, I nodded. He whispered to me, 'Walk away from it, Rachel. Walk away. Be happy.'

I just looked at him.

* * *

Bannister Close was quite unchanged. The lines of solid, sober houses had bright flowers in their squares of garden. There were no wheeling, calling sea-birds, no sounds of the tide cascading against unyielding rock. Two London sparrows perched on a fence-post.

But the house that was 'home' suddenly was snug and inviting, to match the warmth of our welcome from Doreen and Greg — from assorted neighbours, from Dawn and Robbie who paid a flying visit.

Dawn whispered to me the exciting news that she was pregnant and we must soon go on some shopping trips together. Everyone kept saying Sam and I looked so very well, and Sam had grown still taller. She announced with pardonable pride, 'I wasn't sick even once all the way home! — was I, Ray?'

'Not once!' I confirmed. It had been a near thing, but this strangely matured Sam had somehow held out — I believed because she considered we were unreasonably ejected from Gull Cliff, and she wouldn't give them the satisfaction of causing another horrendous journey.

For all I chattered and laughed, explaining that Rick's thrilling new prospects naturally meant abandonment of his 'time-filler' book, I knew both Doreen and Dawn suspected some big sorrow. When my friend left she whispered to me diplomatically, 'So — will you still be keeping in touch?'

I shook my head. 'No. Dawn, I don't want to talk about it — or him. Not yet.'

To Doreen I said even less. Very kindly she didn't press for details. She didn't even — as she was entitled to — voice a triumphant 'I told you so.'

I laid down that night in my own familiar bed. My own room, my own home, my own world. In the morning, we went to The Willows for a happy reunion: it was a delight to see my father's face light up, to see Sam hugging him and eagerly helping open his presents. After that, she vanished through Miss Crocker's front door, armed with a model lighthouse made of shells and enough lurid tales to astound the little music teacher.

As well, we visited the music-orientated school I had mentioned, St. David's, and were able to acquire a glossy prospectus. Sam glanced at the photos of young violinists and pianists and a woodwind class, and muttered only a disparaging 'Huh! — it's not the same.'

Well, nothing would be quite the same as studying with Rick Corelli. I believed she would come round. And with his substantial cheque in the bank I went ahead and arranged an interview for her. Before the day of Doreen and Greg's departure it was actually settled, and we went shopping for yet more school clothes.

With various trips to shows and London sights, it seemed the last few holiday days were a whirl. I didn't sleep, I tried not to think back — I chattered too much and laughed too much. The house that was home, the life that was mine, became totally absorbing. Far away were the fairy-tale beauties of St. Denna, a man's voice, a man's lips warm upon mine.

The day came all too soon to escort Doreen and Greg to the airport, to face more goodbyes. We *must* come out to them to stay during next summer.

Doreen insisted, no arguments, no excuses. Something exciting to look forward to. Something to cheer me up a little . . .

'I'm sorry it went wrong for you,' she confided to me finally. 'I haven't asked you, but I know it did. Ray, it's probably for the best. You've all your life ahead.'

She meant well. No-one could really understand.

It was a very subdued Sam who started the Autumn term at St. David's scarcely interested in the new school, still nursing her own sorrows. Without her I found the house in Bannister Close unbearably empty. I was numb, numb . . . and lonely, lonely . . . and quite fiercely I told Dawn. 'Please, look out for another job for me! — any job!'

'More typing? Are you sure?' she asked with obvious doubt.

'Typing — waitressing — child-minding — dogsbodying — I did the lot at Gull Cliff! Any sort of job, so long as there aren't any famous pianists involved.'

'Point taken. I'll keep my eyes open,' she promised.

It was the first day of October, with a chill mist in the air and leaves falling early to tread damply underfoot, when I met Sam from St. David's as I mostly did. The handsome red-bricked building was spilling out its pupils in their distinctive grey and pale-green. Sam was definitely growing taller, I thought as she walked alone through the throng, her serious eyes downcast. Her hair was pinned up in a twisted plait, and it suited her. Her face looked older, more assured — and sadder. I thought of the childlike Sam I took to Cornwall, just a few months — or was it years? — ago.

'Nice day, Sammy?' I asked, receiving into the car her school-bag and music-case.

'Um. I had an extra music hour with Mr. Fischer, he's quite nice. Not a bit like . . . but fairly nice. Oh, and I got all the maths test wrong.'

'Well, that's not the end of the world! There's some news — Dawn rang, I've a job interview with a Professor Someone who's researching local history. And a letter came for you, I think it's from Mariella.'

That lighted a spark of interest as I steered out into the afternoon traffic. I wondered, as so often before, whether I was doing the best thing for this so beloved young sister . . . whether St. David's was right for her, whether I should have done more to help her secret hurts. Or could anyone really help them?

'Look at these leaves coming down,' I commented as we turned into Bannister Close. 'Mrs. Williams' tree is almost bald already! — '

'There's a big van,' Sam said. 'Outside our house.'

There was a van, a large drab-coloured one. There was also an irate driver and his bored gum-chewing mate: they had evidently been ringing my bell and were consulting a clipboard of papers.

'Sorry!' I scrambled from the car. 'Were you wanting us? Is it a parcel?'

'Not exactly a parcel, love. Didn't you get your delivery advice in the post?'

I heard Sam in the background let out a sort of strangled gasp as a document was displayed under my nose: 'Miss Thornton — Blucher Piano — Tuesday p.m., right?'

Sam dug me violently in the ribs. 'It's from Rick! — he promised he'd send it, when we said goodbye!' The decorous sad-eyed schoolgirl of a moment ago was agog with excitement. 'He *promised* . . . but I thought he'd forgotten, or — or he just didn't want to bother . . . '

'He didn't forget, Sam! — he did bother!' a completely new voice confirmed.

It was a familiar voice. In the stress of the moment I hadn't noticed another car squeezing in behind mine, a tall figure beside me on the pavement. As I looked round at Alex Corelli his sudden appearance was as incredible as the object I discerned now in the van, a tell-tale shape beneath its protective sheeting.

'Don't faint, I'm not a ghost,' Alex was saying now. 'Looks like I'm in the nick of time! This is a spare piano, it's been in storage at the practice studio in London . . . when I found out from Gran what was happening I thought I'd better whizz round here in case I could help . . . '

'Well.' I found my voice at last. 'You needn't have troubled. It can go straight back to the studio. I can't possibly accept it.'

'Rachel, it's not for you. It's for Sam. Look at her,' he said softly, 'look at her face. How could you say no?'

I looked. He was right, of course. My sister's gift couldn't be snatched away from her.

There followed the problem of inserting a gleaming grand piano — albeit in the 'baby-grand' category — into our Bannister Close domain . . . a slight problem Rick wouldn't have considered. With wheels, trolleys, a convenient passageway to the rear, it was just possible to shift the instrument via the patio doors into the house. We might well need in future to eat our meals off the mantelpiece.

The sweating vandriver seemed glad to be rid of his freight and of us. I wasn't sure whether to laugh or cry.

'I didn't tell you, it was a secret,' Sam was still explaining, now in breathless awe. 'He said — he wanted me to have it, it needs lots of love and care — or else it would be left all deserted and lonely, he said . . . '

Not just your spare piano. Rick. Not that alone.

'Well, shut the front door!' I said abruptly. 'Everyone in the road must be in hysterics about a quart going into a pint pot! . . . Alex, it was nice of you to call in — will you have some coffee before you go?'

'Please,' he assented.

He followed me into the kitchen, and there drifted out to us snatches of music as Sam tried out her new treasure. She called to us. 'It's — just *heavenly*!' I called back, 'Good!' The presence of Riccardo Corelli was suddenly real and near, filling the house, stirring the pain within me.

My fumbling hands dropped a cup. Alex said quietly, 'Sit down. I'll do it. You've had quite a shock.'

'Yes, I have. I never did receive that 'delivery advice' — or I'd have told them . . .'

Far distant was the big kitchen at Gull Cliff where we had laboured so often together. In this warm familiar little room I hunched at the small table, trying not to break down completely. I watched Alex stirring around. I heard his pleasant voice talking on.

Mrs. Nicholson was well, he said, and busily ordering the Bassetts around. He had himself now removed to a small North London flat, and the new

Accountancy partnership of Parsons & Corelli was up and running. Georgie was in drama school. Liz was happily engaged to her Stevie — and Mrs. Nicholson had sent her already a very nice wedding gift.

All of that was just a preliminary to what came next. Rick and Abigail were still staying with Rick's American friends — but were now looking around for a place of their own. Jade and Jenna apparently were thriving. Rick was already engrossed in preliminary work on the film project — busier, livelier, once again more fulfilled. He had also paid a first visit to the eminent surgeon: it was much too soon to know if anything would come of that.

'There's more.' Alex added. He set down a cup in front of me. 'If you really want to know — Abbey has received a ring. She chose an emerald, I believe. I gather she'll become Mrs. R. Corelli No. 2 around Christmastime. The twins will be bridesmaiding in fairy-tale dresses. The

Italian Corellis will be there en masse . . .'

'Will *you* be there?' I blurted out.

'I'm not sure if Rick will want me. I'm afraid it's still the easy way out to blame me for Tina. But Gran is flying out next month to make sure everything's organised properly.'

'She is? At her age?'

'She'll be ninety about the same time as the wedding. *Don't* let her know I've told you!'

I nodded. I wasn't really even thinking about the remarkable old lady. My mind was forming all the pictures I hadn't dared contemplate until now — and yet, in some strange way, I felt better for knowing the inescapable truth.

'Yes, Gran will have to make the best of 'that girl' in the family,' Alex reflected. 'In a way, it might all work out quite well. They'll spend a lot of time in America — and Italy. Abbey is clever and strong-willed and inventive, she'll keep Rick working and busy come what may. She'll probably cope with the twins like she copes with everything. You could say she's as hard as nails — but that's *necessary* with Rick . . . '

I looked at him silently across the little table. Now there was a shake in his voice.

'You see, Abbey won't be hurt like you would be . . . and Tina was . . . and I was. Ray, I gave all my life to my brother. I'd have done anything in the world for him. It — it broke me up that he believed Tina and I were — '

For a moment the words trailed off. The clear ice-blue eyes meeting mine were bright with their sincerity, brighter still with brimming tears.

'There was *nothing* between us. I swore it to him — and I swear it to you. The reason he found us so often alone together — Tina was very unhappy, very insecure, she kept coming to me for help and advice . . . I didn't want to take sides, I couldn't help her much.

I did what I could. Dear God, it wasn't nearly enough . . . '

His voice finally broke. And it was then that strangely the roles of the two of us were reversed: I reached across to cradle his hands comfortingly in mine. Kind hands, gentle hands. Not Rick's gifted hands that had poured out a tide of wondrous music — and left so many people to drown in the backwash . . .

I said with sudden glaring insight, 'Alex, you loved Tina! — didn't you?'

'Yes, I loved her. I've never admitted it to anyone in the world — I wouldn't say it to anyone except you. I want you to know all the truth. There were times I was torn apart. Oh, it was all so ugly! — he accused me of robbing him, and I did help myself from his account, but it was money I'd earned that he refused to pay me. He broadcast far and wide that I was a cheat and a thief — I'd led his wife astray, I'd stolen his money . . . and of course people took his side, the family believed it because — Rick is Rick and

I'm always just the brother . . .'

'I know. Like I'm just the ex-secretary,' I whispered. 'Alex, we — we're quite a pair, aren't we?'

'Are we? No, sorry — you don't have to answer that.' He had all the vivid emotion of a moment ago in check now. 'I think I'd better go, don't you? Maybe I'll see you around. And I'm sure poor old Sam will enjoy that piano, she deserves it! — '

It had to be that moment that my sister poked a radiant face round the door, far too excited to realise the scene she was interrupting. She clamoured, could she run round and tell Miss Crocker about the piano? — and could Miss Crocker come round to see it?

'Yes,' I agreed. 'If you like. Tell her to bring a shoe-horn if she wants to get into the house.'

'And can I thank Rick? Can I write today? How long will a letter take? — '

'You could phone him, if it's that urgent,' Alex suggested. 'Try this number, you might be lucky.'

'Can I really? Do I just dial it? Ray, can I — ?'

I waved a helpless hand in the direction of the telephone. She grabbed the paper from Alex, we both listened to her voice in the hall quite absurdly prim and correct: 'Good afternoon — or whatever it is where you are. I want to speak to Rick, please — Mr. Corelli . . . it's Sam Thornton in London and it's very important . . . ' Then her voice changed completely. 'Rick, is that you? — this is me! Oh, the piano came! . . . Yes, it's here, and it's just *wonderful* . . . '

By mute and mutual consent, Alex and I shut the kitchen door, clattered crockery, remarked on the autumnal weather. It was a few minutes before Sam reappeared, pink-cheeked and ecstatic.

Alex asked, 'How is he?'

'He's all right! He's seeing that doctor man again next week. He had a huge row with the film director, only Abbey put it right . . . I told him about St. David's, and he was pleased . . . oh, and he gave me a message for you, Ray!'

I whispered, 'Did he ask to speak to me?'

'No, he didn't. He just gave me a message. He said — ' She screwed up her face in concentration. 'He said, 'Tell Rachel hallo . . . tell her I think of her often . . . tell her, please forgive.' In that funny way of his, you know? — that's what he said! And now can I run round to Miss Crocker's?'

Again, I waved a helpless hand.

The street-door slammed behind her. The two cups on the table had long grown cold. Through the window the chilly sky was darkening into an early dusk.

Alex said, 'He did a lot for Sam. And you did a lot for Jenna and Jade. Well — I'd better be going.'

It was strange that after all the time I had spent with him I seemed to be seeing for the first time the man who looked out of those kind, caring eyes. I couldn't explain that. I knew only that I didn't want him to go. As he turned to the door I cried out almost in panic, 'No, please! — not yet! Don't leave me here alone with . . . '

'With what?' he asked quietly.

It was another question unanswerable. Did I mean alone with the piano that was like a ghost of Rick's presence? Or alone with a broken melody, a wounded heart?

'I still love him! If — if he's happy, I'm happy for him. But — Alex, how can you stop loving someone?'

'I never found the answer to that. I can't tell you.'

In my sea of emptiness, now there were warm comforting arms enclosing me. For a moment I held on to him like an anchor in those deep dark waters.

He had loved Tina, he wept for her still. I had loved Rick — with a tempestuous glory that could never be repeated, his nearness that had filled my heart, his face that had gladdened my eyes, his music that had lighted up my soul.

That was yesterday. Tomorrow was

an unknown still to come. As Alex softly smoothed the hair back from my forehead. I looked into his eyes and saw the caring tenderness now open and unhidden. I felt the human warmth of him, his strength, his understanding.

'Rachel, I can't answer what you asked me. I can only say, I never believed I could love anyone after Tina — until I met you. So you see, it can happen! You've been very hurt, we both have, and — we both need to find out if — if there's really Life After Rick . . . '

Just faintly he smiled. Just gently he was still caressing my hair.

'It might take us both a while to find out about that. But we could do some of the finding out together . . . if you think it might help?'

I looked up at him with eyes still blurred by the tears we had both shared. I found I could give him back in answer just a small, hesitant, watery smile.

I said, 'Yes, it might help, Alex. I think it might.'